SHE GOT IT BAD FOR A CHICAGO HITTA

HALO & STORM

Marina J

MARINA J

ACKNOWLEDGEMENTS

HUGE shout out to my whole team over at Miss Candice Presents. You guys are the truth and keep me motivated all the time. Miss Candice, you're the real MVP, and I've never had a publisher like you. I can't wait to see what big things you have in store for all of us at MCP. I'll always follow your lead.

DEDICATION

As always, my books are dedicated to my kids and husband. Thanks for always supporting me.

SHE GOT IT BAD FOR A CHICAGO HITTA

Prologue

THE BEGINNING

Walking into the church, everything was a blur. Tears fell heavily down my eyes, and although my eyes were covered with my signature Gucci shades, everyone saw them. The thing was, I didn't give a fuck. My everything was laying in that casket at the end of the aisle, and I didn't know if I could face her.

I failed her. I should've protected her. I should've been there to make sure nothing happened to her. When the word came to me, it rocked me to my knees. Nothing my niggas could say or do could ever take away the pain I felt. For that shit, niggas had to die.

I was runnin' up in houses and killin' whole muthafuckin' bloodlines behind this shit right here. My girl, my wife? Niggas touched her, so they had to pay. There was no way I was about to sit back and let this shit go.

I struggled to get down to the front of the aisle. Each step got harder and harder. I felt like my Louboutins had cement on the bottom of them. I finally stood in front of the

casket, and I broke the fuck down. Storm looked so fuckin'
beautiful. I leaned over to kiss her and damn near passed out.

I needed my girl. I clung to the edge of her casket
flanked by all my day one niggas. True reached out to me and
touched my shoulder. I turned to look at him, and he gave me
a slight head nod. I straightened up and looked to where he
motioned. My blood began to boil.

"Fuck is you doin' here, bruh? You think shit is a
game?"

"Nun like that, Halo. Just paying my respects."

"Fuck yo' respect. Pay me in blood, my nigga."

"Is a fight really what you want?"

"Fuck a fight. This shit is war!" I roared.

I watched as Deuce walked out with his weak ass
entourage. That nigga always thought he had one up on a
nigga, but tonight, he'd find out different. I wasn't about to
play with nobody. I don't know why niggas always wanted to
test my gangsta. I turned back around to my girl when True
leaned into me to speak. This nigga knew just what to say.

"We doin' that tonight?"

"And you know it. Nobody sleeps, eats, or breathes
the right way after tonight. Whole bloodlines, my nigga.
Start with his mama."

"Bet that."

Chapter One

The Faction

The Chi has four parts to it: North, South, East, and West. The city is so big that you could never visit every single part of it even if you lived here your entire life! There were four heavy hittas in the Chi. We all knew our boundaries and lived in harmony for a long ass time, until Deuce took over the South after his pops passed away. Ever since then, the nigga been a pain in my fuckin' ass. Every time I turned around, this nigga was causing drama everywhere I turned, and that wasn't good.

Me and the other heads decided to have a sit-down. This was how things were always done. Shit was passed from generation to generation. The rules stayed the same--respect the boundaries, get your work and weight up and don't create unnecessary drama. So far, myself and the other two heads stuck to the law. Deuce was the only one tryna change shit. That wasn't flying with us.

When I entered my warehouse, security was in position, and everybody was in attendance except for Deuce's worrisome ass. I didn't have time for his shit today, and neither did the other two heads. I shook hands with Bread and Butta before I took a seat. These niggas and they corny ass names. I laughed at that shit every time I thought about they asses. They lived up to their names though.

Bread's shit was makin' him a guap. Butta's shit sold so smooth that the nigga was sellin' out of fifteen keys a week. I couldn't knock their hustle at all. We took our seats and waited on Deuce to show up. All of us were agitated because this nigga was always late for everything. We just wanted peace and to continue to run the city like we wanted without the police interfering, but lately, Deuce been fuckin' up.

Deuce waltzed his ass in twenty minutes late with four niggas with him. He knew the rules and wanted to be a dick about it when security stopped their asses.

"Man, fuck off my people. They with me. Swole

ass, fake ass nigga."

"Deuce, you know the rules, my nigga. Either they go outside, or you're excluded from the meeting." I snapped.

"Who the fuck died and made you king, nigga? I do what the fuck I want when the fuck I want. I say they stayin'."

Before Deuce could understand what was happening, all his boys were lit the fuck up. That's what I paid security for. He looked around in astonishment before glaring back at me. He mugged my ass all the way to his seat. I nodded at Bo, the swole ass nigga Deuce was talking shit too, and he started to clean up while we started our meeting. Bread spoke first.

"All my numbers are up on the North. Product is good and no drama my way. I'd like to keep it like that." Bread glared at Deuce.

"Over East is good. Everything smooth like butta, baby. No drama my way either."

"Out West is hittin'. We doin' numbers on top of numbers. No drama my way."

We all looked at Deuce waiting on him to speak.

"Fuck y'all lookin' at me for? I'm tired of all this shit. Y'all up here tryna act like the fuckin' Black Mafia in this bitch havin' meetings and reportin' numbers. Fuck allat! I ain't doin' this shit no more."

"Fuck is you tryna say, Joe? This how shit always been. Either you with the shit, or you dead. Your choice. Your ass can always get replaced." I yelled.

"Man, I swear on my daddy's grave I'ma knock yo' shit back, Halo. You think you badass, but you ain't nothin' but a lil' bitch. You the only one 'round this bitch talkin' all that tough shit, but I bet if I-"

"E-FUCKING-NOUGH! Deuce, on my soul, I swear you actin' like a lil' ass kid right now. You fuckin' up the dynamic, kid. This city is big enough for all of us to eat. You the only one complainin' about the shit. If I didn't know any better, I'd think you was against The Faction." Bread spat.

Bread was the oldest head of The Faction. Then came Butta, even though they were twins, then me and Deuce. You could tell that he wasn't with the shit

Deuce was spitting. Real talk, none of us was with the shit. In due time, Deuce would be replaced, but that was something me and the other heads would talk about without his presence. It was high time he was gone. Too much drama and police meant that drought season was approaching, and if there's nothing I hated worse than a bitch ass nigga, it was a drought.

A drought meant no money and too many antsy ass people. People like that were liable to be on some shady ass shit. I knew for a fact that I didn't want to have to murk nobody, but I would in a heartbeat. Nobody put any fear in me, including any of the niggas sitting at this table. Deuce hopped out his seat and tore out the warehouse like a little kid throwing a tantrum.

"You know he's gonna have to go and soon, right?" Bread acknowledged.

"I agree. Nigga makin' too much noise. Noise brings problems. Problems bring police. I'ont like that shit." Butta put his two cents in.

"I'm with y'all on that. You know how we do shit though. Is it a unanimous vote?"

Everyone shook their heads.

"That's it then. I'll get the specifics together and find his replacement. This shit won't be easy because the South is the biggest part of The Faction. There's gonna be a lot of niggas willin' to go to war with us over that shit." I relayed.

"If it's a war needed in order to end the bullshit, then so be it. I'm 'bout to be too old to be doin' this shit soon anyway. I can do this one time for the last time," Bread said.

"A'ight. Once I get everything figured out, I'll call a meeting. Until next time, fellas."

I shook hands with Bread and Butta and watched them leave. I sat in my chair firing up a Newport, inhaling it slowly. I stroked my chin as I thought about what we had to do in order to keep the balance between all of us. I had no clue when Deuce decided to go rogue, but the nigga was wildin'. Fucked up thing about it was, I grew up with Deuce. He knew me just like I knew him. He was the only one that knew about the real me.

"Yo, Halo. Fuck is you still sittin' there for? We ridin' or nah?" my nigga True asked me.

I got up, slapped hands with him, and went out the door. I walked over to my old school Chevy and got in. True always rode shotgun with me, and today wasn't any different. He was my right-hand man, my brotha from another mutha. He was my best friend. We did everything together. We dug out our first chicks together, sold our first bricks together, and now, he's with me running my side of town, together. I am my brother's keeper.

I gave True a quick rundown of the fuck shit that Deuce was on. He was thirty-eight hot when I was done. Everybody knew his ass was bad for business, and it was time to take care of it.

***

"So, how we 'posed to take care of this nigga?" True asked.

"Same way we take care of every other nigga that always went against the grain--whole bloodlines, my nigga. Deuce ain't no different. He already knows what's up. He gotta know that he can't keep doin' this shit and thinkin' we 'bout to let shit slide."

"Facts. You got an idea of how you wanna

handle it?"

"Not yet, but I'ma come up with a plan. For now, I wanna see if he's gon' hang himself or not."

"Bet."

"Eh yo, drop me off at this lil' broad's house."

"Damn nigga, ya' dick gon' fall off with all these random bitches, my dude. You need to settle down."

"Fuck allat. You know I'm all about the money. A bitch can only get a nut outta me these days."

"Look, I get that was some foul shit happened, but it's still plenty of bitches out here that'll be down for you. Stop punishing yourself, bro."

"Can we not talk 'bout that shit? It ain't even necessary."

I just let the conversation drop. I knew that shit was a sensitive subject for bro. Kalila was a sore subject for him. After that shit happened, my nigga wasn't the same no more. I dropped him off where he asked me to and headed home to my girl. I was in need of some pussy really bad after the day I had, and Storm had the remedy. I could go for a shower, some food, a blunt, and some pussy; in that order. I cruised I-290 headed home with my girl on my mind.

Chapter Two

True

After Halo dropped me off, I was kinda pissed! It took a long ass time for me to get over Kalila and what happened with her. That shit still plays heavy on my mind. She was 'IT' for me. She had a banging ass body with a pretty smile. The funny thing is, her eyes is what made me notice her. Shorty was inside the mall when I peeped her. Both of us were in Foot Locker copping the new Jordan's when I overheard her talking to her friend about her work.

I listened to shorty go on and on about how she couldn't wait to open her rec center. Her eyes lit up when she was talking about all the kids she wanted to help. She said something about showing them that they didn't have to become products of their environment. I was the worst product of my environment, and I knew shorty was probably out of my reach, but I decided to shoot my shot anyway.

I stopped her, and we talked briefly. She eyeballed me in a way that most women didn't. Most bitches saw me and saw dollar signs, but she looked at me differently. I was young wearing nothing but designer labels. I had on the freshest J's and a Rolex with an iced-out bezel. Shorty knew I had money.

"So, what's good, ma? Can a nigga take you out or somethin'?"

"First off, hello. How are you? My name is Kalila. What's your name?"

"Oh shit, my bad. My name is True. I'm doing fine. How are you?"

"I'm doing well. True, huh? That's your real name or your street name?"

"Straight to the point, huh? I like that shit. Yes, it's my real name. It's what my mama put on my birth certificate. I don't know why she named me that, but it is what it is," I said shrugging.

"Give me a reason I should let you take me out," she said standing there with her hands on her hips.

Damn. I just wanted to kiss all over her. I was feeling like one of them corny ass niggas that had to be all in they feelings and cry like Drake and shit to get a girl. Shorty had me off my square, and we hadn't even been talking for long.

"Well, I could tell you some dumb shit, but I ain't cut

like that. I think you're beautiful and want to get to know you better. Can I do that?"

Kalila blushed, and next thing I knew, we were exchanging numbers. I was young as fuck back then — 'bout seventeen or so. Me and Kalila were together for six years. Shorty was definitely down for a nigga. It showed in everything she did for me. I remember her telling me she loved me every single time I walked out the door. She had me wanting to do so much different shit. At one point, I was even considering letting all this shit go and being legit just for her. That's how I much I loved her.

The last year we were together, like 2008, was the worst year of my fucking life. Shit was hot in the streets. Halo's pops had passed away the year before leaving everything to Halo. Since Halo's mom had died a while back, it was just them two. I had to have my nigga's back because you know how the game goes. When a legend dies, everybody wants the throne, but Halo was with the shit.

We were in the middle of a bloody ass beef with niggas who were constantly coming for our spot and more specifically, Halo's head. I wasn't letting bro go out like that, so we stood side by side and handled the shit. Just when we thought shit was Gucci, niggas ran up in my spot, killed my girl, and all for nothing. I never kept shit in that house. Kalila wasn't even supposed to be there. I had her at my safe house tucked out in Romeoville. I don't even know why she went back to the house out west.

When I hit my street to grab some shit before heading to Romeoville, all I saw was flashing lights. There was a big ass crowd of people and yellow crime scene tape everywhere. I pulled off to the side and hopped out running. I saw that it was my house and started pushing past everybody. I tried to rush past the crime scene tape, and a cop grabbed me. I punched his ass dead in the face and kept running till I got to the door. Another cop tackled my ass, and I wrestled with him.

I kept yelling that it was my house, and they let me go asking me for some ID. I showed them what they asked and asked what happened. A detective pulled me to the side, and just as he was about to explain, the coroner rolled a body out on a stretcher in a body bag. He paused after introducing himself, but I really couldn't hear shit. My focus was on the body bag. He sounded like the parents off Charlie Brown and shit, but my head snapped towards him when he said Kalila's name.

I ran over to the stretcher after that and pulled the zipper back on the bag. The coroner tried to stop me, but the detective nodded his head at him. When I finally saw the face of the person in the body bag, it was like my whole world stopped. My body got hot like hellfire. There was a single gunshot wound to her forehead. I screamed loud as fuck and dropped to my knees. My heart was in that bag. What the fuck was a nigga to do?

I don't know who said anything, but somehow, Halo showed up. My nigga scooped me up from the ground and led me over to the steps. We both sat silently as the cops moved about. That was the one thing I loved about this nigga. Halo never pressed me about shit; he just let me do my thing. Once all the cops left, we talked. The city was about to be bloody as fuck.

We got the niggas who killed my girl and a few that didn't, but shit was done. After that though, it was fuck bitches and get money. I didn't want to get close to another chick living the life I was living because I didn't want to feel like I did when Kalila was killed. I sent my shorty out like the queen that she was, but it did nothing to console the way that I felt. A nigga was straight ruthless after that. The only thing a bitch could get from me nowadays was a wet ass, dassit.

I walked up to shorty's door and knocked. A few seconds later, she opened the door butt ass naked, and my dick stood up. I liked that type of shit. Shorty snatched me into the house, and as soon as the door was shut, she was down on her knees pulling my dick out my sweatpants. I let her do her thing. This lil' bitch had the jaws of life! She sucked my shit so good that a nigga was about to hit a Mariah Carey high note and shit.

"Oh, shiiiiiitttttt! Suck that shit just like that. Girl. Fuck! Where ya' mama at so I can thank her? Gotdamn! You suckin' the fuck out this dick. Catch this nut."

I let off all in her mouth, and she kept sucking. I stood on my tippy toes trying not to fall. Bitch straight sucked my soul out the tip of my dick. I had to stand there for a second and catch my breath. Shorty tried to get up and kiss me, but I wasn't going for none of that. I turned my head, and she got my cheek. I peeped how she got mad, but I ain't care. I took her by the hand and pulled her into the living room.

I pushed her over the arm of the couch and played in the pussy with one hand while pulling a condom from my pocket with the other one. I wasn't about to be caught up with a lil' freak bitch like that. Shorty knew I had money and didn't hesitate to ask me for some every now and then, but I never gave her shit except this dick. She knew what it was. I slid the condom on tossing the wrapper on the floor and plunged straight into her. She screamed, and I almost forgot how tight she was. She definitely had some good ass pussy and even better head.

I dug her ass out for about an hour only switching positions once to let her ride me. She tried that kissing shit again, and I almost knocked her ass off me. I would've done it, but my nut was about to come, so I just turned my head again. She got mad and started wildin' on the dick. I came a few minutes later and tapped her on the thigh so I could get up. Walking with my hand secured around the condom, I went straight to the bathroom. I went inside, flushed the shit, and made sure it was gone before washing my dick and hands off. I turned around to shorty standing in the doorway.

"What's good?"

"Why do you do that to me, True?"

"Do what?" I asked, playing stupid.

"You know what I mean. Every time I try to kiss you, you turn your head. So, I'm good enough to fuck and suck you, but I can't kiss you? I thought you was my nigga."

"You thought wrong, shorty. I never said you was my bitch. You just assumed you was."

"That's real fucking foul, True. You been fuckin' with me for like four months now. What kinda shit is that?"

"That's real shit. I never take you anywhere. I never break bread with you. I never buy you shit. Peep the signs, shorty. We just fuckin', dassit! You wishin' for somethin' that ain't gon' happen."

"You know what? Get the fuck out my house. You really ain't shit for that. All this time I'm thinkin' we tryna build some shit, and you tellin' me that this ain't that. That's fucked up on so many levels. I ain't goin' for this shit. Bye, nigga!"

Shorty stomped off, but I didn't even give a fuck. I got what I came for, so I was about to be out. A nigga didn't even take his shoes off, so that should've let her know what the deal was. As I scooped up my phone, she came stomping back into the living room mean mugging me. I found that shit funny.

"You really mad about that shit, shorty? C'mon. You really thought we was together? What you on? A nigga didn't even buy you somethin' off the dollar menu. You should already know what I was on."

"Fuck you, nigga. Niggas like you always think bitches are on some get money type shit, but all of us ain't the same. You just like the rest of these niggas out here. You thottin' it out with all these hoes, but can't wife a real bitch."

"Thottin'? Now that's funny, and a real bitch? Ain't came across one yet. You wildin', shorty, and it's not a good look."

"Why you still talkin' to me? Get the fuck out my house!" Shorty yelled.

"So, what you sayin' is, I can't get one more for the road?"

Shorty tossed an ashtray at me, and I ducked. I left out the house laughing at her ass as she cussed me out. I gave no fucks though. I called one of my people to come scoop me up, so I could get to the crib. A nigga needed a hot shower, a blunt, and some food. I was tired as fuck, and busting two nuts didn't help either. My homeboy came and got me, stopped me by a restaurant, and dropped me off at my spot.

I headed inside with my food laughing about the shit with shorty. It was so fucking funny to me how she got mad. Who the fuck thinks they 'bout to be wifed, and I ain't never even took her in public? That's why I was on good bullshit with these bitches out here. Fuck every last one of them. If they weren't Kalila, then I didn't want 'em.

Chapter Three

Halo

I made a mental to note to check on True in the morning. I shouldn't have brought Kalila up, but I knew that was on his mental. That shit with Kalila hit all of us hard as hell. She was part of the squad. She had been around as long as Storm. It hurt like hell to see bro go through that shit and know there was nothing I could do to help him. It was what it was though. I parked and got out hitting the alarm.

When I unlocked the door, I opened it up to rose petals all on the floor. I heard the music playing. I loved how Storm knew how to get me relaxed without me even having to say anything. It was like shorty vibed with me on a whole 'nother level. She had shit set up so sweet. Had a nigga like me feeling all soft and shit. I rounded the corner and saw the sexiest shit ever.

Storm was sitting on top of the kitchen counter with nothing on. She had her legs spread wide with a smile the same way. When she saw me, her face lit up, and I went straight to her. I pulled her into my arms, and she smelled so good. It was like some type of Vanilla and flowers type of fragrance. I pulled back from her and licked my lips.

"Damn bae, talk about welcoming a nigga home."

"I knew you had your meeting today and thought you might need a stress reliever, so I decided to have this together when you got home."

"I swear you the fuckin' best, bae."

That was another thing: Storm knew everything about what I did. There were no secrets between us. I knew that what we had was a lifetime thing, so I wasn't worried about her snitching or anything. Storm climbed down off the counter and led me by my hand to the table. I was so caught up in her that I didn't realize the table was set. I sat down to a plate of steak, broccoli, and a fully loaded baked potato.

While I ate, Storm sat across the table from me eating a bowl of fruit. The way her lips wrapped around the strawberry she was holding had me ready to tear her ass up. I hurried to finish my food, so I could take her upstairs and tear my dessert up. I pushed the plate away full as hell and stood up. I took Storm by the hand and led her upstairs. She had catered to a nigga enough. Now it was my turn to cater to her.

I stripped out of my clothes as soon as I walked into our room. I watched as Storm walked over to our bed. Her ass was thick, and her body was on point. From the top of her head to the bottom of her feet, shorty was stacked. Her chocolate skin was the most beautiful part of her besides the obvious. Her ass was just as big as her titties, but it was proportioned just right. Her thighs were perfect. My eyes traveled her body as she lay down on the bed.

I walked to the edge of the bed and pulled her towards me by her feet. I took her left foot and kissed each toe sucking on them slowly. I knew she liked that shit. I continued with her right foot, and she moaned loudly. I tapped the bottom of her foot, so she would look at me because her eyes were closed.

"Play with that pussy, bae. Make that shit super wet the way I like it."

Her hands went straight to her pretty little pussy, and her fingers worked up a frenzy. I took my time kissing up the insides of her legs up to her thighs. I pushed her hands to the side and replaced them with my mouth. Her groan was deep and guttural. I sucked on her clit before licking up and down all in her pussy. Storm grabbed my dreads and pushed my face into her pussy. Now that was the nasty type of shit I liked. I went crazy after that sucking and slurping her pussy up like I was thirsty. She was cumming in no time.

Her legs were still shaking when I stood up and grabbed my shirt to wipe my face off. I tossed the shirt down and tapped her to get her attention.

"Give me a minute, bae. That shit felt soooooo fucking good! I can still feel it."

"Ain't no waitin'. Get yo ass up and get the strap!" I barked.

Storm was a little freak, so she hopped her ass up quickly. She went into the closet and came back out with the strap. She passed it to me and hopped back on to the bed. I grabbed her arms and pulled them behind her back. I tied her hands up quickly with the strap and made sure it was secure. Her ass was tooted up in the air just the way I wanted. I stood behind her and slid right into her tight hole.

"Ssssss, damn, bae," Storm moaned out.

I stood inside of her not moving. Shit felt so fucking good. I grabbed her hips and worked her middle. She couldn't do shit but take it. I grabbed her by the back of her dreads and pulled her to me.

"You like this shit, don't you?" I whispered into her ear.

"Yasssss bae, yasssss. Oh, my gosh! Fuck me!"

I long-stroked the fuck out of Storm. "My lil' freak bitch like that shit?" I asked her.

"God yasssss. Halooooooo!" Storm yelled out.

I spent the better half of an hour stroking the shit outta Storm until she creamed all over me. The control shit heightened my orgasm. Before I knew it, I was cumming everywhere, and so was she. When I pulled myself away from her, she stayed where she was trying to catch her breath. I removed the strap from her hands, and she fell flat on the bed. I smiled and went into the bathroom to get her a washcloth. I cleaned myself up first then went to her to do the same.

Storm fell straight to sleep laying on my chest. I held her close and let my thoughts linger. The shit with Deuce was heavy on my mind. I didn't wanna take his ass out, but he left me no choice. The days of old was how I handled my business. Pops taught me well. I ran shit just like he did before he died. I kept his legacy alive by running shit the same way. I fell asleep with my woman sleeping peacefully and my thoughts swirling around. I had to come up with a solution and fast.

***

"Halo....Halo! Wake yo' ass up, nigga!"

I jumped up shaking my sleep off and saw Pops standing at the foot of my bed. I grabbed my shorts and slid them on over my boxers. Nigga had me shook as shit. I hated when he did that shit.

"What you want, Pops?"

"Nigga, who you buckin' at? Remember who the fuck I am!" he roared.

"Damn Pops, chill yo' ass out. What's up?"

"That nigga Deuce gotta go, kid. What you plan on doin'?"

"I really don't know, Pops. You know we go way back. I'm kinda skeptical 'bout shit. I think he just actin' out."

"If you leave the door open for doubt then all kinds of shit will creep in. Handle that shit before it goes too far."

"But Pops, Deuce knows me and my secret. What if he decided to expose that shit?"

"Fuck that secret shit! How the fuck I raise you? After ya' mama died, I did the best that I could. You 'bout as thorough as any nigga out here. Why you questionin' shit?"

"I'm just saying, he knows me."

"God knows you, so fucking what! You know you, right?"

"Hell yeah!"

"Ok, then. You my blood. My seed. My muthafuckin' legacy. Time to put in work. Shit is dead, Halo. Handle that shit."

I woke up around four in a cold sweat. Shit like this scared the fuck outta me. Even though my dad was gone, he always came to me in my dreams, especially when I was having a hard time dealing with certain shit. He just confirmed that I had to handle Deuce, and I would. I lay back in my bed thinking about the shit that went down that caused my father's death.

A lot of people thought I was being too nice after my pops died, but it was all about planning. Deuce and I had literally grown up together. When I wasn't at his house, he was at mine. My dad had been grooming me for his position since I was a kid. I stayed by his side since I didn't have my mom. She died after she had me. She was going through some post-partum depression shit and killed herself. I didn't know what happened to her until years later when my pops told me. I felt some kinda way, but there was nothing I could do about it.

Pops was beefing tough in the streets with some no name niggas. They came outta Cleveland thinkin' they was about to take shit over in the Chi. That wasn't happening. Pops tried to be diplomatic at first inviting the niggas for a sit-down. They refused which was a slap in the face to my pops. It was war after that, and he took to the streets. The night my father died, I'll never forget it.

I just came in from school. I was about seventeen. I tossed my book bag next to the table in our foyer and called for my pops. He came down the stairs and was suited up. I already knew what it was. Pops had planned for this day, should it ever come. He looked me dead in my eye and nodded his head. I was far from weak, but in that moment, I felt my weakest.

The cops knocked on my door a little after midnight and let me know that my father had been killed. I reacted the way anybody would knowing that their only parent was dead. I fell out on the floor after being informed, and the cops just walked away. I don't know how long I stayed on the floor with the door open, but I finally picked myself up. I planned my pops' funeral and sent him out like the king he was.

Everybody in the city of Chicago came to pay their respects. I sat on the front pew with my signature Gucci shades on. I didn't let a tear fall in front of any of these niggas. True sat to my left ever observant. Deuce was to my right on the same shit. We were bred for this shit, but all of us didn't think we'd ever see this day till long off in the future. My father was a fuckin' Chicago legend! I went through the whole service numb as fuck.

When we got into the family car to ride to the cemetery, I replayed the last conversation I had with my father.

"Halo, you know what this might mean tonight. Just know that me and your mother loved you to death despite what you might think."

"I know that, Pops. Do you really have to go though? I already lost Moms, I can't lose you too." I sobbed loudly.

"Look at me. LOOK AT ME!" Pops bellowed. "I do this shit for you. Ever since ya' mama killed herself, I always told myself that I'd do anything necessary for you. All of this was always for you, Halo. You are my heart in human form. You are what I live for. You are who I'd die for. That might happen tonight. I prepared you for this a long time ago. Just take my spot and avenge me, Halo. I love you, kid." My pops said, pulling me into his embrace.

I felt like such a little kid in that moment, but I couldn't stop shit. I did what he said and prepared myself. Once the funeral was behind me, I set forth to get the niggas that killed my pops. By any means necessary was the idea. Whole fuckin' bloodlines was how I was doin' shit. I wasn't about to give anyone a chance to come back at me for shit. I slaughtered every nigga and their families that had some shit to do with my pops' death. After that, it was smooth sailing.

After my pops died, I assumed his position the same way everyone else took their spot except for the twins. Bread and Butta earned their shit and rightfully so. Their pops was only over the North, but Butta took over the East with no problems since there was no leader there. Everybody fell in love, and there was harmony in the city. Now Deuce done fucked it up for everybody, and because of that, we had no choice. He had to go.

Chapter Four

Deuce

This nigga Halo was irking my whole soul. Muhfucka laid down four niggas from my crew like shit was cool. Halo was gon' have to see me for that shit. There was no way in hell I was about to let shit slide nor was I about to let Halo keep being on this king shit. I was finna kill all that shit, starting with Halo.

If there was one thing I learned being around Halo's pops, it was that everybody had a weakness. I knew for a fact that if anything happened to Halo's girl, Storm, that would be it. I was ready for war though. Halo could bring any and everything and still wouldn't win this war. Halo would die just like Pops did. I was with the shits from the moment my people got laid down. I wasn't even too worried about Bread or Butta, but I had a plan for them too. Just from times past though, I knew they didn't get into beef that wasn't theirs, so I was purely confident in the fact that I could get rid of Halo and still play my part before fully taking over the whole faction.

I pulled deeply from my blunt as I thought some
more. Dee came up behind me placing light kisses on
my neck. I shook her ass off me. I swear, this bitch
should know enough about me now to know not to
touch me when I was pissed off. I heard her smack her
lips, so I turned around to face her.

"What, man?"

"Don't what me, nigga! Every time you come
home in a foul ass mood, you wanna take that shit out
on me. I ain't did shit to ya' ugly ass! You better learn
how to leave that street shit outside."

"Yo, who the fuck you think you talkin' to?"

"I'm talkin' to yo' monkey ass! Ain't nobody else
in this damn room but me and you, muthafucka!"

Dee did this shit every time. When I was pissed,
she knew better, but she stayed with the shits. I knew
what would fix that shit. She was in need of some dick,
so I was about to lace her ass. I grabbed her by her neck
and backed her up to the wall. She grabbed at my
hands, but I squeezed a little tighter. I used my other
hand to search under the shirt she had on to snatch her

panties off. She had none, so that was even better. I hiked her leg up and played with her pussy.

Her hands went from my hands at her neck to my belt. She unhooked it in seconds and had my dick in her hand stroking it. She rubbed the tip and spread the pre-cum all over it. I pulled my dick away from her and shoved it into her waiting pussy.

"Shhhhhhiiiiiittttttt!" she screamed.

"Shut that shit up. Take all this dick, bitch. You ain't talkin' shit now, is you?"

"Fuck you, Deuce. You ain't shit, nigga."

"I'm not shit, but you love this dick though. I can feel yo' ass cummin' now. Nut all over this dick."

I fucked the shit outta Dee until she passed out. She had a mouth like a nigga, and sometimes, I wanted to slap the shit outta her, but that was my baby. I loved her lil' feisty ass. She was my motivation behind what I had planned now. Even though we got into it, she held me down. When I took over the South, she was riding shotgun with me. She was setting up traps with me, collecting money, and laying down disloyal niggas for me. She was a rider for real. I owed her that much to take her to the top with me, but make no mistake about it, she could go too if the bitch got disloyal.

While Dee slept, I rolled another blunt and sat thinking about how I was about to fuck the whole game up. I had a crew of thirsty lil' savage niggas who were trained to go. We were getting ready to hit a few of Halo's traps in the next two days. I had planned to hit Halo where it hurt the most. The four traps I was planning on hitting were Halo's most profitable. If I could get rid of those traps, then that puts a dent in Halo's pocket.

I finished my blunt and tossed the roach in the ashtray. I laid back in the bed with Dee snoring loudly. I rolled her over on her side so she'd stop snoring, and I could get some sleep. I put my hands behind my head and sat in deep thought. I needed all this shit to go off without a hitch and without niggas knowing that it was me who set the shit up. I needed all those niggas in The Faction to be none the wiser that it was all on me. I fell asleep on that note.

***

I woke up a few hours later feeling refreshed. I

took a shower and got myself together. I was ready to get back to the money because it was definitely calling my phone. I saw that I had over a dozen missed calls and hella text messages. I bypassed the few I saw from Halo and went straight to the ones my lil' nigga Drop sent me.

Drop: I bn sittn' at da spot jus watchn....whatchu u want me 2 do?

Drop: Halo done bn thru...follow or nah?

I hit him back real quick and told him to sit at the spot. I needed to know how shit was running through there. I hit up Kilo, Zane, Bose, and Core to check with them. I had Kilo on another spot. Zane was at the one on the border between the West and South sides. Bose and Core were together at the most lucrative spot on Washington near Pulaski. I had to do this shit with precision.

I grabbed my keys, put my phone in my pocket, threw on my Chicago Bulls snapback, and was out. Dee was up and around this bitch somewhere, probably sitting in the living room with that damn kindle reading. She loved all them hood stories and shit and was friends with a ton of authors on Facebook. She followed their asses religiously, especially the company, Miss Candice Presents. I can't even lie, some of those books were good as shit. I peeped a few of them when she would leave the shit laying around. Those chicks was beasts when it came to writing.

Just like I thought, when I hit the bottom of the steps, she was curled up on the couch with a blanket draping over her legs and her kindle. She was laughing at some shit. I walked over, kissed her on her forehead, and let her know I'd be back later. She waved me off and told me she loved me. That's all a nigga had to hear before I left. As long as my shorty was good, I was good.

I hopped in the whip and turned on *Gangstaz Don't Live That Long* by Lud Foe. I cranked it up and sped out my parking spot. I headed into the city on the way to the money. It was a good ass day to fuck some shit up, and that's what I was about to do. First, I had to make sure my shit was secure before I hit Drop and told him it was a go tonight. It was the first of the month. Tonight those traps would have the most money--more money than they'd probably see all month.

The fiends were out in full effect when I hit the city limits. Today was a good day indeed. I anticipated just how much money was in Halo's houses. My hands were itching because of it. That meant money and a lot of it too. I ran through my spots and locked shit down. Everybody understood what they were to do, and I let them know I'd be back later to get my money. That was a crucial part of my plan. If I was seen making pick-ups when Halo's shit got ran through, nobody would suspect me for shit.

I stopped to get some food. While I waited, I texted all my lil' niggas and let them know we needed to meet. I had a lil' unknown spot near Cottage Grove right off 63rd Street that nobody knew about. It was a building that I owned, but it was in Dee's name. It had some apartments in it, but they sat atop a storefront. I used that for a base and where I stashed all my shit at. Nobody knew that I kept all my money here. The safe that I had was state of the art too. Not only did it need a code, but it had a hand and eye scanner too. I wanted to make sure nobody could get into my shit.

I killed my food and headed over to my building. I was there for only ten minutes before my crew showed up. We all slapped hands before we got down to it.

"So Drop, Kilo, Core, and Bose, I need y'all to hit the first spot Drop was watching today. Bose, make sure the car is ready to go when they come out and keep watch for any niggas lurking. That spot on Lockwood and Division has a lot of foot traffic over there, so y'all gotta be in and out."

"We layin' everything down, right?" Drop asked.

"You already know what it is. Not a soul lives. Murk 'em all," I replied.

"Bet that. I'm ready."

I went through the specifics with them one more time. I let them know where I'd be and where we'd meet back up at tomorrow. Just in case something were to happen, they were to text me 911, and that let me know to meet them back here. Only in an emergency were they supposed to come back to this spot. I didn't expect anything to happen, but you never know. We chopped it up for a few more minutes before I sent them on their way.

Chapter Five

Storm

I woke up after the amazing sex session Halo,
and I had last night feeling great. Halo was the fuckin'
best! I remember when I first met Halo. I was In North
Riverside Mall with a few of my girls. I wasn't buying
anything because I had more than enough shit.
However, I couldn't help but indulge. I had money,
and I was smart with my shit, but every now and then,
I splurged on myself.

I had a few bags from Forever 21 and was
headed into Charlotte Russe because I saw something
in the window that I wanted. As I was walking in, I
heard a group of loud ass niggas. I stopped in my
tracks and saw Halo. We locked eyes, and it was like
nothing or nobody else mattered. It felt like my soul
was attached to Halo's in that moment. I looked Halo
up and down assessing everything.

Halo had a sexy peanut butter complexion with

perfect teeth. I saw dimples and dreads, two things I was a sucker for. On Halo's feet were a pair of fresh Balenciaga high tops. Balmain jeans and a plain white t-shirt fit Halo's frame loosely. Halo swaggered over to me with that million-dollar smile, and that was it. We'd been together ever since then. Halo was the love of my life, and I couldn't wait until we got married.

The one thing I loved about my boo was the fact that we had no secrets. Anything Halo was involved in, I knew about. I was the stress reliever for my baby on many nights, and I didn't mind that. If there's one thing I knew for sure, it was the fact that I handled my business when it came to my relationship. Halo already knew what it was when we got together. I tried to play hard to get, but that shit didn't last long at all.

Halo swept me off my feet, and within a year, we had moved in together. We've been together for almost seven years now. Kalila was my best friend. When she was killed, I saw what it did to True, and that's when I started to fear shit every time Halo left the house. When I told Halo how I felt, there was no hesitation in pacifying me. That's why we had a house built in Romeoville. No one knew about it but True, and that's how we wanted things. I stayed in the house we had in the city a few days a week, but most times, I was at our main house.

Halo handed me a duffle bag full of money and told me to go shopping when our house was complete. The house in the city belonged to Halo's parents. There was no selling it; it was where Halo grew up. There were still pictures everywhere of Halo's parents and even his grandparents. This was the house I wanted to raise our babies in, but when I voiced my concerns to Halo about all the street shit, that's when the other house got built.

Sometimes I thought about Kalila and what we'd be doing if she were still alive. True was like a brother to me. When he got with Kalila, I knew they'd be together forever like me and Halo. Never in a million years did I think she'd get killed. She was supposed to be my maid of honor in my wedding, Godmother to my babies, sister to me for life. But, she was gone, and my brother was a mess fucking with these hoes out here with no feelings.

I got up, relieved my bladder, and turned the shower on. While I waited for it to heat up, I checked myself out on the mirror. I was a bad bitch, and I knew it. I had a body most women die for, and it was all compliments of my mama and my grandmother. I was cornbread thick. Everything was proportioned just right. I turned around to look at my ass, and that's when Halo walked in and smacked my bare ass.

"Owww, nigga! That shit hurt," I said rubbing my booty.

"My bad, bae, lemme kiss it for you," Halo said, bending over to kiss my ass, literally.

I pushed Halo away from me knowing that if we got started, we wouldn't stop. I got in the shower, and Halo left out the bathroom to make some calls. I took a long, hot shower. This felt so damn good. When I got out, Halo was gone, but there was a tray of food on the bed with a little love note. It made me smile because Halo always did shit like that. That's how I knew our love was real. I ate my food and thought about my baby. This was life.

I finished eating, threw some clothes on, and

headed to the kitchen. I cleaned my dishes and got dinner in the crockpot for later. I headed straight to the dining room that I had turned into a mini office. We didn't eat in here, so I made this the base of my business. I had products everywhere. My business was popping. I had several products that I had created for people with dreads. There weren't enough products on the market for us to use, so I made my own. It was tedious work, but I worked at it until I perfected it.

I had worked out a distribution deal with several big chain stores like Walmart, Target, and Sam's Club. My hair products were sold everywhere you looked. I wasn't stressed over money. I think that's one of the things that impressed Halo the most. I had my own money and was doing well when we met. I never had my hand out because I had my own bag. Whatever Halo gave me was just a bonus.

I sat at the computer and checked my emails for orders. There were a few other female entrepreneurs that I worked with. They promoted my brand, and I promoted theirs. Right now, *Be Smooth Bands* by Jay J and *Saphirre Beauty* by Saphirre Aviles were popping just like me. We traded products back and forth and promoted each other on our social media accounts. I loved uplifting other women when it came to securing the bag. Girl power was the shit.

I reviewed a few orders, sent out some invoices, and did some inventory for a while. I packaged up a few things so I could head to the post office and send them out. Once all my business was handled, I got myself together so I could go get my nails and toes done. Halo loved that shit, and I always made sure my nails and toes were the same color. Halo had a foot fetish and loved sucking on my toes, especially after I just got them done. I checked myself out in the mirror before grabbing my Michael Kors purse and the packages I needed before heading out. I locked up and tossed everything in the back seat of my royal blue Audi A8 and was out. I went to the post office on Division and Lavergne. I always used that post office because they knew me there.

I sent emails to my clients after sending their packages and headed to the nail shop. The wait wasn't long, and I was in and out. I drove back towards the house needing to get a few things before heading out to Romeoville. Halo told me to go straight there after I handled what I had to handle in the city. I don't know why, but I had a really bad feeling for some reason, and I couldn't shake it. All I could do was hope that Halo was alright.

I got to the house, grabbed my things, and was out within minutes. I just made it to my car when I was hit from behind. I fell to the ground, everything spilling out my hands. I tried to turn around to see what the fuck was going on and was hit again. I felt dizzy, and my vision was blurry, but I tried to get up once more. I was hit again, and I felt myself about to pass out. What the fuck was going on? I succumbed to darkness after I was hit repeatedly.

***

I woke up to the sounds of hushed voices and beeping. I tried to shake my head, but there was too much pain. I moaned out and winced. I heard Halo near me.

"It's ok, bae. Just take it easy."

"What the fuck happened? All I remember is

somebody attacked me, and now I'm here."

"I called you earlier to see if you made it out to the house yet, but you didn't answer. At first, I didn't think nothing of it, but something told me to call you again. I called you five times, and you never answered. I remember you put that Life 360 app on my phone so we'd know where each other was at at all times. When I saw that you was still at the house in the city, I went over there. I thought maybe you just decided to take a nap or something. When I got there, you were laid out on the ground bleeding and shit. I was so scared, bae. I brought you straight here. They looked at me like a nigga beat you because of the condition you were in."

"Somebody came up from behind me and hit me. I don't know how many damn times. I kept trying to get up, but they kept hitting me."

"Did they say anything?"

"No, they just kept hitting me until I couldn't get up."

"Whoever did this shit crossed a line. People know who you are to me. Muthafuckas think shit is sweet, but I'm 'bout to fuck the city up over you. I need to know who was this fucking bold."

"Bae please, can you just leave it alone? I'm scared something might happen to you."

"I can't do that. Don't you know how much I love you? Violating you is like a slap to my face. The disrespect is real! I can't let this go. What if this would've been worse? I don't know if I could get over it if anything happened to you like what happened with Kalila." Halo looked at me with tears threatening to fall.

More than anything I wanted Halo to see that seeking revenge wasn't worth our lives. I just wanted to live in bliss with my baby and go about our lives. I wanted to make beautiful babies and live happily ever after. I just needed Halo to see that. This whole thing wasn't worth it.

"Halo please, do you love me?"

"More than anything in this world."

"Then please let this go."

"I can't promise you that, bae."

And with tears streaming down my face, Halo walked out of my hospital room. My heart broke in that moment because I knew Halo wouldn't let this shit go. I couldn't help but worry what our lives would be like from this point on.

Chapter Six

Halo

More than anything, I wanted to do what my girl asked of me, but I just couldn't. The fact that this could've been a lot worse is what had me scared as fuck. Thugs get scared too, fuck you thought? As if this shit wasn't enough, while I was waiting for Storm to wake up, True texted me. Somebody hit my trap on Division and Lockwood. That was one of my big money makers, so I was pissed.

Once I knew that Storm was ok, I left. I had a lot of shit on my mind. I was thinking heavily of what Storm asked me to do. I headed in the direction of Division Street to see what kind of damage was left behind. I barely got to the block when I saw all the flashing lights and police cruisers. The whole damn block was cordoned off. I had to park on Laramie and walk over.

A few people saw me and nodded showing respect. I nodded back and walked to the edge of the crowd. People talked, and I wanted to see what they had to say. I listened as murmurs went through the crowd.

"I saw the shit when them niggas pulled up."

"It was like five niggas I ain't never seen before."

"All I heard was *pop, pop, pop, pop, pop, pop*. They ran up outta there fast as fuck."

"I saw the whole thing, but I ain't tellin' fuck ass CPD shit. I need to get in touch with Halo."

I walked over to the guy who made the last comment. I tapped him on the shoulder and motioned for him to walk with me. He looked shocked but followed me. We headed back in the direction of my car. If he saw everything like he said he did, I needed to know what he knew. We got to my car and got in. As soon as his ass hit the seat, he started talking.

"Man Halo, them niggas pulled up in a fuckin' minivan. Four niggas ran inside, and one stayed in the car. I never saw them niggas before a day in my life!"

"If you saw them again, would you recognize them?"

"Hell fuck yeah! What you want me to do if I see

them again?"

"If you see them again, call me at this number," I said writing my number down. "I got five stacks for you when you do."

"Bet that. Good looking out, Halo."

I dapped dude up, and he got out my car. I was beyond heated. My girl got beat up the fuck up, and now my trap was outta commission. Fuck my life right now. I guess this is what my pops felt like when all that shit went down. I vowed to not let myself go down like my pops. All I had was Storm, and I didn't wanna leave her alone in this fucked up world. My girl was my everything. If I was gonna start a war, I had to make sure my army was just as strong as me.

I drove off headed towards True's spot. I needed a blunt badly and didn't want to smoke around all these fuck ass cops. They'd pull a nigga over quick just because. I got to the apartment that True rented and stayed in when he was in the city. I parked and used my key to go inside. Something told me I should've just knocked, because when I walked in, this nigga had his meat shoved down some chick's throat, and the hoe didn't miss a beat.

"C'mon, man. You knew I was coming through. Have 'ol girl bounce."

"Give me a minute, bro. I need her to catch this nut right quick. Fuckkkkk! You suckin' the shit out this dick, girl. You earnin' that rent money for real."

I walked off on that nigga and went into his kitchen. This nigga was a damn fool. He was in there hyping that girl up like she had the ball and just took the game winning shot in game six of the play-offs. I heard the door shut a few minutes later, and he came strolling in the kitchen with a smile on his face.

"You're a fuckin' idiot, bro. Earning her rent money, huh? How much you broke her off with?"

"Hell yeah! She earned every bit of that one-hundred-and-thirty I gave her."

"Wait a damn minute. How much is her rent?"

"That bitch on Section 8. Her rent only twenty-one-dollars a month. She said she was behind one month but wanted a few extra dollars for herself, so I gave her a little extra because she made a nigga see Jesus when I busted that nut. Her ass better not come back for six months with that rent bullshit."

"You're a fuckin' idiot, bro," I said slapping my forehead.

"Wassup though?"

I sat down and told him what happened on Division. He was just as pissed as I was. I also told him about homeboy who told me what he saw. I knew that True would find a way to find out who did this shit. If there was one thing messing with all these hoes did for him, it was get him information. They stayed telling my nigga shit just to be able to be in his presence. He pulled his phone out and shot off several texts. A few minutes later, his phone beeped.

Thottie South: I got some info for you, Daddy.

"Yo, this lil' hoe I fuck with from out South said she got something."

"So, hit her back, nigga, and see what she knows," I said irritated.

He shot a text back, and within minutes, 'ol girl hit him back.

Thottie South: I'ma need some dick & some cash, but I know who hit y'all trap.

I told him to have her come through so we could get down to business. Whoever did that shit was as good as dead anyway once I got my hands on them. Shorty said she was on the way, so we waited. She got there like forty minutes later thinking she was about to get broke off by both of us, but I shut that shit down quick. I had a girl and wasn't fucking around on her. I got what I needed and dipped. I let True handle his business with her.

I don't know who those niggas were, but since they were from out South, I could only speculate at the time. I knew Deuce had something to do with this shit. There was no way around it. He was causing more and more trouble every time we turned around. Shit was getting old fast. I hit the expressway and headed back towards UIC Medical Center where Storm was at.

I parked my car in the parking garage and went inside the hospital. I got my visitor's pass and headed straight to my baby's room. She called me earlier, but I couldn't answer because I was handling that business with True, but I was all hers. I swear, once this shit was over with, I was gonna take my girl on a vacation, and we were getting married. I couldn't spend another day without her being my wife.

I stepped into the room and saw that Storm was asleep, so I took a seat in the chair next to her bed. I rested my head on the bed as I leaned forward and grabbed her hand. I was so pissed right now! Why niggas had to touch my girl? Why couldn't they just leave shit alone? I fell asleep thinking like that. Maybe an hour later, I felt Storm's hands in my dreads. I moaned and stretched before looking at her.

Storm was looking at me with tears in her eyes. She knew what it was about to be. I knew she was scared. She knew that at any moment, this life could snatch me away from her. I needed to make her feel safe, secure, and stable. I decided that I'd keep my ass home for at least a week when she got out of here. I stroked her face in my hands and kissed her softly.

"No talking, baby, just listen. I love you, and I know I can't really promise that I'll never get hurt. What I can promise is to love you with every breath I have in my body. I wanna marry you, girl. Say yes, and I'll go get you a ring right now! I want you to know that no matter what, I'll always love you and take care of you."

"Bae, I love you too. You really wanna marry me?"

"Hell yeah, like yesterday. Is that a yes?"

"That's a hell yes! Yes, I'll marry you. I love you so much, bae."

"SHE SAID YES! WHOOOOO! MY GIRL SAID YES!"

The nurses came rushing in to see what the commotion was.

"Excuse me, what's going on in here? It's very late, and we have other patients asleep."

"I'm sorry, but my girl said yes. She's gonna marry me." I gushed full of joy.

Everyone clapped for us, and we finally settled down. I climbed into the bed next to Storm and held her all night. This was it right here. This was what I wanted. I was done as soon as I handled them niggas and got shit squared away with True. He could have this shit. I fell asleep next to my soon to be wife, and I was good.

Chapter Seven

Bread

Normally, my brother and I keep to ourselves. This shit with Deuce though was draining all of us. I knew without a shadow of a doubt that he had to go. Butta and I were on board with Halo on getting rid of him. The shit that pissed me off was the fact that he thought he should be the one running things. Who the fuck died and made his ass king? The shit we had worked for us. It was the way all our people before us did it.

Halo's pops, our pops, and Deuce's pops all ran together back in the day with this one other cat. When he died, the responsibility of his side was up for grabs, and that's when me and my twin stepped in. After our father died, I took over the North, and Butta stayed taking care of the East. Shit was smooth and had been that way for a long ass time. Me and my twin were older than Halo and Deuce by a few years. That's why we didn't care for all that young nigga shit.

When I got word of what happened out West, I called Butta. He had already heard. We both hit Halo with a text for a meeting so we could get rid of this nigga once and for all. I would bet every last dollar that I had on the fact that Deuce had something to do with that shit. Nigga was straight reckless. I was waiting on a text back from either my brother or Halo. While I waited, I stared at my sexy ass, sleeping wife.

Beauty was a nigga's dream. Of course, her real name wasn't Beauty, but that's what she was to me, so that's all I called her. She stood at five feet even. Her chocolate skin was flawless. From the top of her head to the bottom of her feet, everything was perfection to me. She rocked a short haircut, and I loved that shit. Her body, shit, her body was off the chain. 36-24-48, baby was stacked. I was so in love with my wife, and she with me. Lil' baby was the truth!

Beauty had been down with me for almost fifteen years now. She met me when I was a lil' ignorant ass nigga on the block thinking I was hot shit. I was feeling myself and just knew I could get any chick I wanted, and I wanted her. When I approached her, she acted completely unbothered by me. Most broads were throwing the pussy at me, but not Beauty. She laughed in my face and walked away. Every time I saw her, I tried to shoot my shot, and she shot me down every single time. She was hard to get.

I want to say that over time I broke down her resolve, but honestly, I'm not sure what it was that made her finally give me a chance. She said it was my persistence. I say I'm just lucky because she's the best thing that ever happened to a nigga. I knew one day she'd be my wife, and five years later, I slid a ring on her hand in the wedding of her dreams. We said our 'I do's' in a church full of family and friends and honeymooned in the Caribbean hopping from island to island.

We had two sets of twins. One set of boys and the other was a boy and a girl. My daughter, just like my wife, had me wrapped around her little finger. And rightfully so, they were the only women in my life. Anything they wanted, they got. My sons were little replicas of me. As soon as Beauty told me she was pregnant, I was ecstatic! I got a house built far the fuck away from the city. I didn't need my family in jeopardy because of what I chose to do. Even though I knew Beauty could bust a gun with the best of us, I never wanted her to. Thankfully, she hasn't had to.

Our house was all Beauty's doing. She designed everything. As a matter of fact, that's what her degree was in. She graduated from Chicago State University with a degree in Architecture. Our entire house was a blueprint she made with the intention of having a big family one day, and it was her dream house, so I made it happen. She deserved that shit too. Anything her heart desired, I gave it to her. She was my queen, and I would die for her.

My street shit never came home with me. At home, I was just daddy to my kids and Brandon to my wife. My sons didn't know what I did in the streets, and my daughter thought I was a superhero. I did everything in my power to keep them away from what I did outside our home. Damn, right I was sheltering them. As far as they knew, daddy was a boss who could do whatever he wanted to do, and he had a lot of money. My family was my everything.

Halo finally hit me back, and right behind that text came one from Butta. Shit was a go, but first, we had to find this lil' ignorant ass nigga. Knowing the type of shit he did, he was probably hiding out somewhere with his girl. I didn't like that bitch either. I didn't even disrespect women, but she was a bitch in the truest form. All of our women had tried to befriend Dee, but her whole vibe was off. None of our women wanted anything to do with her, and that was rare for all three of them not to like Dee.

I remember the first time Deuce brought Dee to a little function we put together. We all sat together, and the shade was real as fuck. Dee kept making little slick ass remarks about all our women, and I guess that my wife had had enough of it. Beauty snapped on her ass, and after that, Deuce never brought her around again. At least his dumb ass knew better than to let his girl get her ass whopped. The shit he was on now though, I didn't know what he was thinking.

I slid from underneath Beauty and got dressed. We were on a mission tonight. I threw on my hoodie, grabbed my phone and keys, kissed my wife, and left.

The fifty-minute drive to the city would be enough quiet time for me to relax and get in my zone. Me, Butta, and Halo needed to get together to come up with a plan. I hit a few people up earlier today to secure a few things. By tomorrow, everything would be set. We just had to find these niggas.

By the time I reached the city limits, I was faded off the Kush blunt I had smoked. I was focused as hell. I made it to our meeting spot and parked. As I was getting out my car, I got a call from a lil' dude off my side.

"Yo Boss, you ain't gon' like this shit."

I pinched the bridge of my nose knowing this was about to be some bullshit. *"What's good?"*

"Trap got hit when I left to take the money we made to the drop house. It's cops galore out this bitch. The whole damn street is blocked off, and somebody said everybody is dead. I'm standing off to the side of the crowd now, and they already brought out two body bags."

"Fuck! Any word on who mighta done this shit yet?"

"A nigga in the crowd said they saw four niggas run inside and one nigga in a minivan sitting outside."

"You already know what to do. Lemme handle some

shit, then I'll be on my way. "

"Bet that."

I hung up more pissed off than I already was. I stormed towards the building with murder on my mind. When I walked in, my phone chimed. I opened up the message to see it was from my young one. It contained five names. That was all I needed to start the bloodshed that was sure to occur. I dapped up Butta and Halo and took a seat.

"Yo, that nigga Deuce is out of control. I know he's behind this shit," Halo said.

"I already know. I just got a call from one of my young ones. One of my traps got hit too, but they didn't get shit because the money was already taken out the house by the time they got there. I got two dead kids and probably three more inside the house. Only one who didn't get killed was the one who was dropping off the money. He's the one who called me. He said the cops were crawling all over the scene. It's time to shut down shop until this shit is over with."

"Agreed, brother," Butta replied.

"Did your young one find out any info on who

did it?" Halo asked.

"He said it was five niggas in a minivan. I just got a text from him with some names when I walked in here."

"What are the names?"

"Drop, Kilo, Zane, Bose, and Core," I responded.

"Lemme hit True up. Some broad he deals with said she had some info for him," Halo said pulling out the phone.

While we waited for True to pick up the phone, we politicked for a few. True confirmed the names with Halo, and it was repeated back to me. Now it was time to go. Butta was quiet, but he was more quiet than usual. I tapped him on his arm to knock him out of his trance.

"What's good, lil' bro?"

"Some wild shit, man. I'm tryna be focused on this shit here, but I'm kinda all over the place right now."

"I need you focused. Shit 'bout to get real. What we about to do is some crazy shit. I know you tryna go home to your wife alive and in one peace just like I am.

Focus, bro."

"I'm focused, man, but it's like I'm more focused than ever even if it doesn't seem like it. I'm just shocked I guess."

"Shocked about what?" Halo asked jumping into the conversation.

"I'm 'bout to finally be a daddy!" Butta exclaimed, smiling proudly.

"My nigga! Congratu-fucking-lations. Welcome to the daddy club, bro. When did y'all find out?"

"Earlier today. A nigga been floatin' since we left the doctor, and we're having twins too. I hope it's two boys, but even if it's not, I'm still happy as shit."

"I'm happy for you, my dude. I can't wait till Storm has one of our babies."

"One of them? Damn nigga, how many you tryna have?" I asked Halo.

"I wanna whole fucking house full of kids. Like six or eight, shit, maybe even ten. You know all I got is me and Storm now. My people all gone. I don't wanna have just one kid and stop. I want all my kids to always have each other in case some shit happens to us."

I laughed at both these niggas. Baby bro had twins on the way, and Halo's ass was talkin' 'bout havin' a damn Brady Bunch. This was all the more reason to handle the drama in the streets. Last thing I needed was to lose one of these niggas. We got down to business and hatched out a plan. Once we had everything set, I dapped up bro and Halo and left, headed to my trap. I hit my young one, and he told me he had to bounce, but he was at the money spot, so I went there.

It was a quick fifteen-minute ride to my money spot. When I walked in, my young one was suited up and ready for war. He had a gun pointed at the door when I walked in. Once he saw that it was me, he lowered his gun and got up to dap me up. We slapped hands and sat down to talk. He ran through everything he found out and confirmed again that them niggas were from out South. I fucking knew it! Deuce was as good as dead when I caught his ass.

Chapter Eight

Butta

I was the quiet twin--always was. While Bread was more sociable, I wasn't. I stayed watching and observing everything. I came into the world with my twin, and if need be, I'd go out with him. He was my other half, and for a long time, it was just us and our parents. Our mom left our father and us when we were like eight. I remember the night she left because my parents had this big ass fight that woke me up. Bread was always a hard ass sleeper, so he never got up.

I heard something shatter against the wall, and that's what woke me up. I came out my room and was sitting at the top of the stairs when I heard my parents going at it. My mom was yelling at my pops. That shit stayed on my mind for a long ass time after that.

"You ain't shit, nigga! I didn't sign up for none of this! I just wanted to live a lavish ass life, but noooooo, you wanted what you wanted. I tried to love you as best as I could, but ever since I gave birth to them two lil' bastards, you forgot all about me. It was all about Brandon and Brian.

What about me, Brennen? What about me?"

"You selfish as fuck, Jazzy. You're their mother, and you act like you want nothing to do with them. You carried them in your body and gave birth to them. How could you go from the woman I loved more than life to a heartless bitch?"

"Selfish? Heartless? Nigga, that's you! As soon as them niggas was born, you forgot all about me. It was Brandon this or Brian that. You forgot about your fucking wife! What happened to loving and cherishing me? You just said fuck me and gave it to them. I hate you!"

"You ain't gotta stay, Jazzy. Get yo' triflin' ass the fuck out my house. I got my sons! But don't worry, I'll never tell them they had a sorry ass excuse of a mother. You ain't shit."

"Yeah, whatever, fuck boy. You can have them niggas 'cuz I don't want them. I never fucking did. I only had their asses to shut you the fuck up. I was gonna get an abortion, but you found the pregnancy test."

"Fuck did you just say?"

"You heard me. I was gonna abort them lil' fuckers, but you found out. That's why they here, and that's why I hate your ass."

"Because you're their mother, I'ma let you leave with

your life, but you better not ever show your fucking face around here again."

"Good fucking riddance to all y'all bastards."

Our mother never showed her face again until the day of our pops' funeral. The bitch had the nerve to come in crying like she had been a devoted wife all this time. She didn't even get up the aisle good before we were on her ass. I knew what it was. She thought because she was still his wife that she could just come back and reap the benefits of the last decade, but she was mistaken. Me and my twin had been put on game to why she was there.

The way our pops went out was suspect as hell, and we both knew it. After our moms left, we never saw pops with another woman like that. He would smash a chick here or there, but they never came to the house, and he never introduced us to a new woman. He never went looking for our mother nor did he divorce her. She was just gone. We found our pops dead in the foyer of our house. He would never bring anyone there because of us, or you meant something to him. That's when we put two and two together.

Bread told me to let him handle the funeral, so I did. While he did that, I hit the streets and stayed in the shadows. There was mention here and there of Jazzy being back in the city, but she was also rumored to be fucking with Deuce's pops at the time. Just like a snake ass bitch. That nigga was a fuck boy in the truest form. I knew both of them had something to do with my father being killed. Shit fucked my head up when I got confirmation that Jazzy did too. Our own fucking mother.

We snatched her ass up, and of course, she flipped out in the church, but I approached her, and she shut up. She tried to play it off like she was so glad to see me and Bread and that our pops had told her to stay away from us or he'd kill her. I played her little game and took her out to the truck we had our guys ride in for the funeral. I told her to stay there, and we'd talk afterwards. Like the dumb bitch that she was, she stayed put.

I finished out the funeral with my brother and our girls at our side. We buried Pops at Mount Emblem Cemetery. It was like the whole hood came out to see him off. I refused to let a tear drop though. Bread was a little different from me in that he didn't care about showing his emotions. I had a hard time doing that shit, even with Baby. She was the only chick I let get near me after that shit with Moms. Once my father was laid to rest, we sent the girls to the house for the repass and went to take care of dear 'ol Moms.

When we climbed into the truck on either side of us, she played like she was happy to see us. We both knew it was a bunch of bullshit. We drove off headed towards this lil' ducked off spot that we had out near the Indiana border. When we got on the expressway, she visibly relaxed and thought shit was all good. We passed the exit to our house, and she pointed that shit out.

"Didn't we just miss our exit?"

"Nah, we been moved. We goin' to the new house," I responded.

"Oh."

After that, she sat quietly. I could feel the anger coming from my brother. Guess it was that twin shit. I was just as pissed, so I knew he felt it too. We finally pulled up to a rundown looking apartment building. Jazzy looked at us in confusion. Her head swung back and forth between me and Bread.

"What's going on? Where are we?"

"Shut yo' ass up and get the fuck out the car." Bread barked at her snatching her by the arm.

"Boys, I thought we were gonna talk. What is all this? I love you guys. You're my sons."

"Love? Fuck outta here! Bitch, you full of it. Walk,

gotdamn it," I said, shoving her from behind.

She was trapped, and she knew it. She walked sandwiched between us with her head down. She was sniffling and crying, but we didn't give not one fuck. This bitch not only said fuck us and left but turned around and killed the person who loved us more than life. That was the most despicable thing ever to us. She had to pay with her life, and there was no way around that. Bread pushed her towards the lone chair that sat in the middle of the room. The two guys that rode with us started to tie her up for us.

Once she was good and secure, she looked at us with tears in her eyes. Jazzy tried to plead her case over and over, but that shit fell on deaf ears. I was about tired of her talking, but Bread kept telling me to wait. He said he wanted to get pissed off at the realization of everything, and that's when she'd finally tell us the truth. It didn't take too long for that to happen. I think we'd only been there for thirty minutes when she did that.

"So, you'd really kill me? I am your mother. I carried you for seven and a half months. I remember you came first, Brandon, and Brian came six minutes after you. You guys were identical to each other and looked every bit like your father. I love you guys so much."

Still, we said nothing. We just stared at her, and I guess that pissed her off.

"I gave y'all asses life! If I had followed my first mind, neither one of you would exist. Y'all ruined my fucking life! When you two were born, your father forgot all about me, but I never forgot about him. I catered to his every need, but all he cared about was you two. You both make me sick. I regretted the day I pushed you both out my pussy. Life was great till y'all came along."

I cocked my head to the side and was about to snap her fucking neck, but Bread put his hand on my shoulder to calm me down. He already knew how I felt. She wouldn't shut the fuck up either. She kept going on and on.

"The night I left your father, I ran off to find somebody who wanted just me. I didn't give a fuck if I had to play second or none of that shit. So long as a man didn't want me to have no more damn kids. I didn't want shit to do with kids. All I wanted was to live my best fucking life, and I couldn't do that being smothered by your father and you guys. Dre gave me that. I hate all of you!"

Bread pulled his hand off my shoulder and handed me the gun in his hand. He took a step back and nodded for me to handle my business. He wasn't too keen on killing women, but he knew this bitch had it coming. I raised the gun and pointed it straight in her face. Before I could pull the trigger, there was a loud crash behind us. We all spun around guns pulled and aimed. Baby stood there with tears in her eyes with Beauty standing next to her.

"Baby, what are you doing here, and why did you bring Beauty with you?"

"Bae, I'm sorry, but I already knew what it was when she showed up. I couldn't let you do this without me. I knew you would need me after this. She ain't a regular bitch."

"Got damn right I'm not a regular bitch. I'm THAT bitch! Let me the fuck up!"

Baby ran over to Moms and punched her dead in her shit. For every punch she threw, she screamed and yelled at Jazzy. You see, Baby thought I was just one of them young, ignorant ass niggas who wanted a bunch of bitches, but that was far from the truth. It was because of the flaw ass shit Jazzy pulled with my pops that made me skeptical of women, but Baby showed me how solid she was. She was a rider for real. I let her get her shit off because I knew she needed it like I did. It was Jazzy's fault I was so difficult with Baby, to begin with. This was like therapy for us.

I pulled her back and into my arms. She squeezed me

tightly, and I looked at Jazzy one last time before raising my gun. Baby turned around, and I wrapped my hand around her waist. She wrapped her hand around mine, and together, we pulled the trigger. Two shots: one to the head and one to the heart. After that, we both left with our women and left the guys to dispose of Jazzy. Now I could breathe easier and treat Baby like she deserved. My issues were gone with Jazzy, and Baby had just proved once again that she wasn't your average woman.

Bringing myself out of my thoughts, I drove home happy as hell. My baby was having my baby. I made Baby my wife about two years ago. When she proved to me that night how much she loved me, I knew I'd be with her for life. She was a little wild, but I know she loved a nigga and had been patient as hell with me all this time. We'd been together since I was about sixteen. I met her a year after Bread met Beauty. We were nearing thirty, and I decided to stop playing games. Bread and Beauty had been married for four years, and they had two sets of twins. I loved my niece and nephews but was ready for my kids.

I was too happy when Baby told me she was

pregnant. It was like she knew I needed some good news in the middle of all the drama Deuce was causing. I came home the night of our meeting, and she had the mood set. Food was on the table, candles were lit everywhere, and soft music played in the background. She met me at the door in some sexy ass lingerie. She took me by the hand not saying a word and led me to the dining room. She pulled my chair back and pushed me down in it. She straddled my lap and kissed my lips. She fed me my food, and it was the most intimate moment I'd ever shared with my wife. I noticed the food she fed me and stopped her.

"Baby, why is the food little as shit?"

"It's baby corn, baby carrots, an eight-ounce steak, and mashed potatoes."

"Baby corn? Baby carrots? Wait, are you telling me something?"

She sat still shaking her head vigorously. She had tears in her eyes and was staring at me intently.

"You havin' a baby? My baby?"

"Yes," she whispered.

"Dead ass?"

She shook her head, and I jumped out the chair cradling my wife. She had just made me the happiest man in the world. I celebrated by dancing around the room with my wife tightly wrapped in my arms. I said fuck that food and took my wife to our bedroom. I made love to her all night and didn't fall asleep until eight that morning. Today would be all about my wife. I finally fell asleep with my hands tightly secured around her belly. My wife was carrying my seed, and I was happy. My life was complete.

Chapter Nine

Beauty

I had been down with Bread since we were fifteen-years-old. That man just did it for me. Even back then when people tried to tell me I didn't know what I was feeling, I knew he was the one. Did he fuck up? Yeah, he did, but I forgave him for the dumb shit. We were bigger than the bullshit. I had seen him through everything, including the death of his parents. I knew for a fact that we would be together till the day we died. If he decided differently, I'd bust a cap in his ass-- no bullshit.

The life we built together was amazing. I can't say that it wasn't. While Bread ran the streets, I ran the classroom. I aced every single pop quiz, test, and homework assignment that I was given. I graduated at the top of my class and valedictorian. College was a breeze for me, and before I knew it, it was graduation day again. I was graduating Summa Cum Laude with the highest distinction.

Bread was front and center dressed in all-white. Butta and Baby stood next to them in white as well. When my name was called, I proudly crossed the stage with a smile a mile wide. Bread met me at the bottom of the stairs. Because a moderator was helping me down the stairs, so I wouldn't trip, I took my eyes off my man for a minute to walk down the stairs without falling. When I looked up, I was coming off the last step, and Bread was down on one knee.

"I know I probably don't deserve you, but I know that I'd be so lost without you, shorty. Please do me the honor of marrying a nigga. Be my wife."

"Yes!" I shouted.

Bread slid a fat ass rock on my ring finger and swooped me up in his arms. I was floating on a cloud, and nothing could ruin my day. We all went out to eat, and at dinner, I told everybody the good news. I was pregnant with twins. My new fiancé was happy as shit, and for the first time since we'd been together, I felt entirely complete. Life was good. Now here it was, years later, and our life was better than ever. Somebody just had to start some shit. I was past pissed.

Thank God none of our kids were old enough to pick up on certain things, and thankfully, we lived nowhere near the city. We were tucked away in Indiana right across the state line. It was a small community of middle and upper-class families. My family and I fit in, in the diverse neighborhood with no problems. My business was thriving and expanding, so nobody looked at us strangely.

The one thing I didn't want to do was move because of some bullshit, but I had a contingency plan, just in case. I had researched places to live both in the United States and out of the country. It looked like the Carolinas were the place to go for retirees. The housing market out there was great. For what we paid in Indiana or even Illinois, I could get a house and a considerable amount of land for the same price. I would have to talk to Bread about it, but I don't think he'd object.

The last thing I wanted to do was uproot my kids, but I knew that moving South would be the best bet. At least there I knew they'd never have to worry about the type of life their father lived. Both of us had busted our asses to give our children what we didn't have as kids. I'd die before I let that shit be taken away.

Sitting at my desk at work, I was in deep thought when my phone rang. I cleared my throat and answered in my best professional voice.

"This is Paula speaking. How may I help you?"

"Bae, it's me."

"Hey, what number are you calling me from?"

"I had to get another phone because I lost mine. I only know your number like that, so I called you because I didn't want you worried about me. It's just a little bullshit phone till I can get to the store and get a regular one. I know you always worry when I gotta go handle some shit."

"I mean, yeah, I worry, but you could've just shot me a text to let me know you were good."

"Picture that shit. If I woulda texted you sayin' all this, you woulda been mad at my ass, and I ain't havin' that. Happy wife, happy life, right?"

"You think you know me." I laughed. *"But, you're right. I would've been hotter than fish grease."*

"No doubt, so that's why I called. You seem off though. What's up?"

Gosh! I love how this man knows me.

"Well, I was thinking about everything."

"And you wanna leave the Chi, right? If I know you, you been lookin' at other states we can move to and shit, so what did you come up with?"

"I swear I love you so much. So far, the best prospect is North Carolina. The housing market is good. We can buy some land. We can build whatever we want there. I can even open another office there. This would be a good move for us as a family."

"Let me think on it, a'ight? You know I can't leave my brother or his wife like that. That's all the family we got, so I have to get him and Baby on board with this too."

"You worry about Butta, and I'll talk to Baby. Be home by seven for dinner. I'm making lasagna with garlic bread and salad. See you later."

"You know the way to a nigga's heart. I'll be there on time with bells on. I love you too, my queen."

"I love you too, my king."

I hung up with Bread and got back to work. I had a few contracts I had to look over before sending them out. The best thing about being the boss is that you could do whatever you wanted. By the time I looked up, it was going on five o'clock, and I still wasn't done. I tidied everything up and stuffed it all in my briefcase. I had to deal with the traffic, so I could pick up the kids, get home, and make dinner. This was the best part of my life.

I got to the daycare in time and got all my babies. I strapped everybody in their car seats and headed home. While Brandon Jr. and Brennen talked amongst themselves, Bryce was half asleep, and Brianna was babbling on and on in baby talk. I enjoyed the chatter of my little ones as I pulled out the parking lot of their daycare. I called Bread to let him know I was on the way home. As I pulled to the left, I felt something hit my car from the back. I looked in my rearview mirror and got out.

"What the fuck, yo? I got my damn kids in the car, and you just hit me!" I screeched.

"Shit, my bad, shorty," a tall nigga said getting out the car. I didn't give a fuck that he towered over me.

"Were you not watching what the fuck you were doing or where the fuck you were going? Bruh, if one of my kids would've gotten hurt because of this shit, I would've fucked you up." I seethed.

"Check her out, bro. Shorty mad-mad. Like really, what was yo' five-foot ass supposed to do, huh?"

I had to think about the fact that my kids were in the car. Otherwise I would've walked back to my truck and pulled my gun on his ignorant ass. I sucked my teeth at him and asked for his insurance.

"What's it gonna take for this to go away? I'ont have insurance, but I got money. Whatchu need?"

"Fuck your money, nigga. I need that insurance info. Fuck you thought? I ain't one of those types of bitches, so let's do this shit legally."

"Damn shorty, chill. All a nigga is sayin' is that my shit ain't legit insurance wise, but I can pay for the damages. Lemme just give you my info, and once you get an estimate of the damages, you can hit my line, and I'll pay for it."

"Fuck hitting your line. I got my own bag, and so the fuck does my husband. I don't need shit but your information, so I can make this report."

"It ain't that serious, shorty. You high cappin'

for no reason."

"You know what? Fuck it. I'm not about to do this shit with some lame ass nigga who don't know how to do simple shit," I said writing down his license plate number.

I walked away and got back in my truck. I pulled off mad as fuck dialing Bread's number. He didn't answer again, and he had me pissed. I called Butta and got no response either. Just as I called Baby and she answered, my car got hit from behind again.

"Baby, please call my husband and yours right now. Some nigga just hit my car, and the same car is ramming me again. I got the kids in the car with me. Hurry, Sis!" I yelled into the phone hanging up.

I tried to speed up, but the car kept up with me. All I had was a Dodge Caravan, so it was no match for the Chevy Tahoe that was behind me. Normally, I wouldn't drive this car, but I knew I had to pick up the kids today, so I drove the family car. I kept going as fast I could to get my babies to safety. I pulled off on the first exit I saw. I floored the accelerator and busted a right. My car damn near tipped over.

I got around the turn and hit the gas. The car was still behind me. It was like everything went in slow motion. I was speeding through the intersection, and I saw the semi-truck at the last minute. It slammed into my minivan on my side, and we flipped over and over and over again. I remember hearing my babies scream. I remember blood everywhere. I remember trying to get out of my seat to make sure my babies were ok. I just didn't remember blacking out.

Chapter Ten

Baby

When Beauty called me, I thought she'd be talking to me about the Sunday dinner we were supposed to be putting together. I had no clue that I'd have to call our husbands because some fucked up shit was going on. I dialed Butta and waited for him to answer. I knew he was more than likely with his brother, so I didn't have to make the call twice. As soon as he picked up the phone, I started talking.

"Bae, put the phone on speaker because I know Bread is with you."

"Yo, what's goin' on? Talk to me, Baby."

"Beauty just called me and said some nigga rammed the back of her car. She has the kids with her. I can track her phone with the app we got, but I don't know if she's ok. According to the app, she's off I-90 just past the Skyway. I'm about to leave the house now."

"No!" Bread and Butta shouted at the same time. *"You stay at home, and we'll go. As soon as we know*

something, we'll call you."

"Oh, you got me fucked up! Beauty is like my big sister, and those babies are my niece and nephews. Like hell, I'm staying home. I'm closer too, so I can find out if they're ok faster than you can. I'll see y'all there," I said hanging up.

I'll be damned if both of their asses thought I was going to stay at home and wait. Butta had that shit bad, but if there was one thing he knew about me, he knew that I was stubborn as hell. I knew when to listen to what my husband said, and then I knew when not to. I knew this was one of those times to listen because I'm sure it was in my best interest, but I couldn't sit at home and not know if my family was ok.

I became a part of this family almost fourteen years ago. Butta was a hard dude to crack, but I knew when I saw him that he was it for me. He was quiet, laid-back, and real observant. I remember that on our first date he bought me lilacs and my favorite book, *Antebellum* by R. Kayeen Thomas. It was one of those things that every woman looks for when it comes to a man; a man who listens. Ever since then, we'd been together.

It was tough to crack through the wall he built up. I knew he cared for me, but it was like he was emotionless, and I knew it had a lot do with the fact that his sorry ass mama had done his dad, him, and his brother dirty. When his father was killed and that hoe showed up at the funeral, I knew what time it was. I wanted in on that shit.

Me and Beauty tried our best to stay at the repast and take care of everyone else, but we just couldn't. We left Halo and True in charge and went to our men. It felt good as hell to take my frustrations out on that bitch. When Butta raised the gun, I had to wrap my hand around his. We needed to do that shit together, and we did. Ever since then, he'd been doing his best to tell me how he felt about me. It was one thing for him to show me but another thing to tell me. Sometimes, a woman just wanted to hear it from her man.

Once he opened up to me, it was like a whole new world. He was only like that with me in private though. I didn't care about all the public shit. Bitches knew who I was, and niggas respected it. If they didn't then it was nothing for me to check somebody over their bullshit. I was a live wire when it came to those I loved.

That's why I was speeding down I-90 now headed towards Beauty and the kids. This was my family. They meant more to me than anything seeing as I really didn't fuck with my family like that. They always used to make me feel some kind of way because I was the dark one. I was darker than all three of my sisters, and them hoes used to talk shit about me on a regular basis. When we all became teenagers, they grew jealous of me, because even though they talked shit about me, the guys loved me and my dark skin.

My sisters were overly friendly and ran through more dudes than I could count. I didn't though. I was saving myself for someone special, and I found that with Butta. He was my one and only. Them bitches I call sisters, loosely might I add, try to call me now and act like shit is all good, but I don't fuck with 'em. I exited on 89th Street and made a right turn. When I got to the first light, all I saw was flashing lights, police, and ambulances galore. This was not good.

I pulled over and jumped out my truck. I ran straight into the melee, but nothing could prepare me for what I saw. Beauty's van was totaled. I completely lost it when I saw medical personnel working on three of the kids. I pushed past the crowd and yelled at the first cop I saw.

"Excuse me! Excuse me, sir! Can you please help me? That's my sister. I was on the phone with her when she said someone rammed her car from behind."

"Hey, let her through, Jones."

The officer lifted the yellow tape, and I went straight to the other cop who introduced himself as Detective Reynolds. I explained to him what Beauty told me on the phone and let him know that I had already called her husband, and he was on his way. I kept looking over his shoulder at the people working on my family.

"I know that this is difficult so let me give you a quick rundown. When we arrived, the woman who was driving was unconscious. There were four children in the vehicle with her. Upon our arrival, we noticed that three out of the four children weren't breathing. One of the children, the one behind the driver's seat, was sandwiched between the driver's seat and back seat where the car seat was positioned at, at the time of the collision. The fourth child was fine and unharmed."

"Can I please see my nephews and nieces? I need to make sure my sister-in-law is ok as well before I call her husband with an update."

"I'll take you to them. Follow me," Detective Reynolds said.

I followed right behind me hoping that everything would turn out good for us. If not, then I wanted in on whoever did this shit. The first person I saw was Brianna. She was so tiny laying there, and I started to cry. They were poking and prodding her and yelling out shit that I couldn't comprehend at that time. The same thing was going on with Brandon Jr. and Bryce. Brennen was the only one who was ok.

He was sitting in the back of an ambulance with a bandage on his forehead. When he saw me, he damn near jumped off the bed. He was four-years-old and very aware for a little kid. The medic let him come to me, and I cradled him in my arms. I didn't know what to say, so I just held him. As I stood there wondering what would happen with everybody, I heard shouting behind me.

"Fuck what you talkin', bruh! That's my wife's car! Her and my kids were in there!"

"Hey, let them through!" Detective Reynolds yelled towards the officer.

Bread and Butta ran over to where I was standing. Bread took Brennen out my arms and hugged him. Butta came to me and did the same. A few seconds later, Bread's head snapped up. He handed Brennen back to me and went over to the other ambulances where Beauty and the kids had been loaded into. He talked with the medics for a few minutes before coming back to us.

"They're taking the kids and Beauty to Northwestern. I'm going to ride with Beauty. Can you guys keep Brennen with y'all and meet me there?" he asked weakly.

"Sure, of course. Go. We'll be right behind you."

As soon as Bread climbed into the back of the

ambulance, it pulled off. The other three ambulances followed behind the one he was in. The detective stopped us to hand us his car and left us alone. We headed straight to my car with Brennen wrapped tightly in Butta's arms. He was still shaken up, but he was comforted in Butta's arms for the time being. He strapped Brennen in assuring him that he'd be ok before sliding in the backseat next to him.

We pulled off and got back on I-90 heading towards downtown. This whole damn thing was a fucking mess. Whoever did this shit was gonna die. They fucked with the wrong family. We didn't even get all the way to the hospital when Butta's phone rang. I watched his facial expressions as he talked to his brother. When he hung up the phone, he turned and looked at me with tears in his eyes. There was only a handful of times I ever saw my husband cry, and each time, it was because something bad happened.

"No bae, please tell me everything is ok."

"Just drive," Butta whispered.

I almost lost my shit in that car, but I drove careful not to scare Brennen. He finally fell asleep, and the last thing he needed was to wake up scared because I was driving too fast. It took us another twenty minutes to make it to Northwestern. We pulled into the emergency parking and hopped out with Butta getting Brennen. We rushed inside where we found Bread sitting with his head in his hands.

"Bro, please tell us what the doctors are saying," I asked him.

"My wife is in a coma. Brandon Jr. is paralyzed from the waist down. Bryce's left lung collapsed, and he has some internal bleeding. Brianna's got swelling on her brain, and they had to put her in a medically induced coma to help with that. My family is all fucked up, and I feel fucking helpless," Bread said breaking down.

Butta handed Brennen to me and pulled his brother into a hug. That's when Bread lost it. He slumped over in his brother's arms. They stood like that for what seemed like forever while I cradled Brennen and cried. Shit was so fucked up right now. I swear God wasn't on our side right then and there because the doctor came in after we'd been sitting there for two hours and delivered more fucked up news.

"Family for Brianna James."

"That's us, doctor," I replied standing up.

"I'm so sorry, but we did everything we possibly could. After Brianna was placed into the coma, she coded causing us to start CPR. We worked diligently on her for over an hour without being able to resuscitate her. I'm very sorry for your loss. I can have the nurse come to take you and your family back to see her when you're ready."

I stopped listening after he said he was sorry. Hearing the shouts and cries coming from my husband and brother-in-law hurt my soul. Why the fuck did this have to happen?

Chapter Eleven

Bread

I felt like my whole world had stopped. My wife was hurt, my sons were hurt except for Brennen, and my daughter was gone. Somebody was definitely gonna have to see me about this shit here. I hit Halo up and told Halo to grab True and suit up. This shit definitely meant war. I asked Butta and Baby to go check on the boys so I could go sit with my baby girl for a minute. The truth was I didn't want them to see me break down.

A couple nurses came out to the waiting room and led us to the rooms we needed to go into. I stood outside the room my baby girl was in. I was scared to go inside. For the first time in my life, I regretted the lifestyle that I lived. It cost me my daughter and got the rest of my family hurt. I finally pushed the door open. Each step to the bed felt like I was wearing cement shoes. She looked so little laying in that bed.

I got all the way to her bedside, and that was it

for me. I screamed so loud that I was sure everyone heard me, but I didn't care. I cradled my daughter in my arms knowing that this would be the last time I'd be able to do this. I wouldn't see her go on her first date or graduate. I wouldn't be able to walk her down the aisle after threatening the man who wanted to marry her. I would never get to see her have babies and be a grandfather with little ones that looked just like her. Oh, my God! What was I gonna tell my wife?

I don't know how long I was laying there with Brianna, but I felt somebody shaking me. I looked up to see my twin and his wife. Butta put a sleeping Brennen into Baby's arms and hugged me and Brianna. My soul was crushed, and it was gonna be crushed even further when I told Beauty. I had cried more tonight than I ever had in my entire life. I didn't know how I was gonna get through this shit, but I knew one thing for certain, I was done after this. This shit had cost me way too much already.

I let the nurse know that I was ready to make whatever arrangements I needed to, then I headed off to see my wife. I sent my brother and his wife home with my son because this shit was gonna be tough to do. I checked on Brandon Jr. and Bryce before going to see Beauty. I felt like I was walking the Green Mile. There was no coming back from this shit. Now, all that shit Beauty had talked to me about moving down south was registering to me. Once I handled this shit, we were moving.

I got to Beauty's room and hesitated before going inside. The doctor said that even though she was in a coma, it would still be good to talk to her. I pushed the door open and almost fell out. Tubes were everywhere, and the machines were beeping relentlessly. I walked over to the bed, pulled the chair up close, and took Beauty's hand. At first, all I did was cry. It was hard as fuck to get my words out. The finality of everything hit me hard as fuck as I sat there with my wife. I just couldn't bring myself to tell Beauty anything, so I just cried.

I must've fallen asleep because I woke up when a nurse came into the room to check Beauty's vitals. Nothing had changed, and she was still in a coma. I wasn't even a praying nigga, but I prayed like crazy. If

I lost Beauty on top of losing Brianna, I was gonna fucking lose it. I held on to my wife's hand hoping that she'd squeeze it or give me some type of sign. I had no such luck.

I checked my phone to see that everyone had texted me. I didn't even care about none of that shit right now. I called my brother back to check on my son as I got up and stretched. He was restless, just like I was and just as pissed. We talked for a few minutes then hung up. I decided to go check on my sons since Beauty wasn't awake. I let the nurses know where I'd be just in case something happened and made my way to the Pediatric ICU.

I scrubbed in, put a gown on, and waited for the nurse to lead me to where my sons were at. They were in beds side by side. Brandon Jr. was alert and immediately screamed for me when he saw me. Bryce was sleeping. I went straight to Brandon Jr. and held him as best as I could.

"Daddy, I can't move. I can't move, Daddy. What's wrong? Why can't I move?"

Hearing my son ask me that broke all the resolve

I had left. I cried so hard and hugged him even harder. He was scared and shaking. I had to gather myself so I could try to explain to my four-year-old that he was hurt. I took a few deep breaths before I looked at my son. The tears in his eyes made me want to cry even more. Shit hurt, man.

"You were in an accident, son, and you got a really bad boo-boo. The doctor said we can try to fix the boo-boo later, but right now, we just need you to get better. You and your brother."

"Bryce hurt, Daddy. Bri-Bri too. Mommy fell asleep when we go boom. Bryce be ok though."

My son's optimism did little to make me feel better. I let him talk my ear off till he finally fell back to sleep. Once I was sure he was good, I went to Bryce's bedside. He was still asleep. His face had black and blue bruises all over it. There was a tube in his mouth and another in his stomach. To see my kids hurt like this had me ready to kill everybody in Chicago. The nurse came over to check on the boys and let me know the doctor would be coming to speak to me about them. As soon as I sat back down, he came over.

"Mr. James? I'm Doctor Fields. Your sons have been in my care since they were brought in. I needed to speak with you because I need to operate on Bryce to clear the internal bleeding he has in his abdomen."

"Whatever you need to keep my son alive, Doc, do it. I'll sign whatever. Is Brandon going to be paralyzed for the rest of his life?"

"I'll have the nurse bring you the consent forms to sign. As for Brandon, I think with some physical therapy and a lot of love and care, he can walk again. He's four, and at that age, their little bodies are still developing and maturing. I don't see why he won't be able to walk again."

"Thank you, Doc. Were you the one who operated on my daughter?"

"Uh, no, sir. That was my colleague. He's one of the best in pediatrics. I can tell you that he did the best job he could given the circumstances, and we are all very sorry for your loss."

"I appreciate it. Have her bring me the forms right away. I at least want to give my wife some good news whenever she does wake up."

"I'll do that now. If you have any questions, have the nurse page me, and I'll come right away."

I sat back down and pondered over what the doctor said. My son would walk again. Bryce needed surgery. Brianna had the best doctor. My mind was all over the place. I let the nurse know I'd be in the adult ICU with my wife if they needed me. As I walked out, I pulled my phone from my pocket and called my brother again. I needed Baby to sit up here with them and at least here we knew she was safe. I needed to make the fucking city of Chicago bleed. It was time to eliminate niggas who thought this shit would fly.

***

Butta and Baby arrived two hours later. By then, the nurses had checked Beauty and my sons one more time without any change. It was times like this I wish I had more family. I couldn't even ask Halo to bring Storm up here because she was laid up in another damn hospital. Shit was bad all the way around, and we all knew that Deuce had something to do with this shit. I couldn't wait to catch that nigga. I kissed my wife, loved up on Brennen, checked in on my sons, and left with Butta in tow. We had to go meet with Halo and True.

I knew Halo was feeling the same way I did. When you mess with somebody's family, all bets are off. We peeled out in Butta's Charger and headed out West to meet Halo and True. We cruised down I-90 switching to I-290 at the interchange. Murder was on my mind just like I was sure that Butta, Halo, and True felt the same way.

We were all down for the same shit. Deuce messed up the dynamic. We were making great money together, and all was peaceful. He just had to fuck everything up. As God is my witness, I was gonna body that nigga. I couldn't rest until I did. There was no way I could sleep or anything until I was sure Deuce was no more. We met up with Halo and True at True's spot and parked. Once inside, we started putting our plan to work. Deuce was a dead man walking, and anybody in our way of him would die too.

Chapter Twelve

Halo

When I got the call from Bread about what happened with his wife and kids, I felt for bro. I didn't have kids or nothing, but my girl was laid up in the hospital because somebody was on bullshit. We all knew that Deuce had something to do with all this shit. We talked amongst ourselves about what we needed to do in order to flush Deuce's bitch ass outta hiding.

Once we had shit squared away, we all left. True went to go hit some bitch up that he said could get him Deuce's whereabouts. Bread and Butta headed back to Northwestern. I had to go cop a ring and get back to Storm. My head had a million thoughts running through it. All this was crazy as fuck. The only good thing in all this was that my girl said yes. I drove towards the mall, so I could get her a fat ass ring and get back to her.

I made it to the mall, headed inside and went straight to Jared's. I looked in all the ring cases trying to find the perfect ring for Storm. I found one in the last case I looked in. That shit was big as hell with pink and purple diamonds in it. She liked that type of girly shit, so I knew I had to get it. I tried to get the attention of the saleslady, but her ass kept ignoring me. I hated to get ignorant up in here, but she left me no choice.

"Excuse me, I know you see me standing here. What? My money ain't good or something?"

"I'm sorry, but you don't even look like you can afford anything in that case. Maybe you want to look over here where the rings are under $100. That's probably more your speed." The white saleslady said nastily to me.

"What the fuck? Yo, where is your damn manager at? Owner, supervisor, some damn body other than you. Fuck out my face before you get slapped with your racist ass."

I was pissed the fuck off. I guess with all the noise I was making, I stirred up enough to make someone come from the back office. Out walked the sexiest, chocolate thang I ever saw besides Storm. For a minute I almost forgot why I was there. She walked over to me, and I had to pick my mouth up. Shorty was sexy as fuck.

"What seems to be the problem here?"

"Are you somebody who's gonna help me or are you gonna treat me like Jewelry Store Jessica over there?"

"I'll deal with her in a minute. Let me help you first. Did you find something you liked?"

"Yeah man."

I pointed out the ring I wanted and the district manager, Anisa, helped me out. I even threw in an extra grand for all her help before turning to the rude bitch who didn't want to help me in the first place.

"I hope yo dumb ass realizes just how fucking ignorant you are. Just because we don't have the same color skin or dress alike, it doesn't make me any less than you. You're the type of bitch who looks like she's mad at life because she works in a mall. Prolly got the driest pussy ever and Brad bust fucking Becky behind ya back. Do the black community a favor and go play in traffic hoe. White bitches like you make your entire race look bad. Now you have a nice fucking day."

I waltzed out, ring in hand with a few people snickering at the saleslady. Just as I hit the threshold, I heard Anisa tell her that her services were no longer needed and that they didn't tolerate any type of discrimination at Jared's. I wanted to go back in there and salute her, but I knew that would be walking on thin ice. The whole time I been with Storm I ain't never checked out another shorty, but that one was bad as fuck. I had to stay away from her.

I bopped to my car, happy that I had a ring for Storm. She could get whatever type of wedding she wanted wherever she wanted to have it at. It was all about her. I hopped in the car and mashed the gas on the way to my baby. Even with all the extra shit going on, I had a lil' something to be happy about. I made it to the hospital and parked. I went inside with a happy spirit and murder on my mind at the same damn time. Funny how that shit goes.

When I walked into Storm's room, I saw her sitting up and fully dressed. I dropped to my knee in front of her bed and asked my girl again, the right way.

"Will you marry me, bae? Say yes to rocking

with a nigga forever."

"You know I will."

I opened the box of her ring, and she gasped. She held her hand out eagerly as I slid the ring on her finger. I got up and kissed her with everything I had in me. I got lost in the sauce because I didn't even realize the nurse came into the room. She interrupted us by clearing her throat.

"Well, now that the passion has subsided up in here, how about we let you go home?" she said happily.

She passed the discharge papers to Storm, and I stepped back as she signed them. She was already being extra making sure to put her ring on display. The nurse saw it and gushed over it.

"Oh, my gosh! That's such a gorgeous ring. Your honey must really love you."

"Completely in love with me too. I love you, bae," Storm said all smiles.

I helped her into the wheelchair the nurse had pushed in with her, and we were good to go. I couldn't wait to get Storm home so she could rest. I knew if I told her about what happened to Beauty and the kids, she'd wanna go to Northwestern. I just wanted her to chill, but of course, shit happens.

Once we got in the car, my phone rang, and Bread's name flashed on the screen. I answered the call on the Bluetooth and was told that Bryce had to have surgery. The way Storm looked at me let me know that she was about to ask a million questions. I pinched the bridge of my nose ready for it.

"What happened to Bryce? What aren't you telling me? No secrets, remember?"

"Yesterday, Beauty was in an accident. Some nigga rammed the back of her car when she had the kids with her. She was speeding trying to get away from him when her van got hit by a semi-truck. Shit is bad Storm, all bad."

"Tell me, Halo. How bad is it? Is everybody ok?"

Knowing the way Storm was attached to the kids, I knew she'd break down once I told her everything. I had no choice, so I spilled everything. She was in tears by the time I was done, and just like I knew, she wanted to go to Northwestern. I headed that way, so we could check on the family. I hurried to park, so we could go inside. I had to remind Storm that she just got out the hospital herself, so she wouldn't overdo it.

We headed up to the ICU and went to see Beauty first. When we walked in, she rushed over to Beauty's bedside. I dapped up the guys and hugged Baby. Beauty was still in a coma. Storm took the seat on the other side of the bed while all of us stood. I nodded at Bread, and he nodded towards the door. We filed out and into the family waiting room. It was empty, so we could speak freely.

"Any news on that nigga Deuce?" I asked.

"Nah, but I got 'ol girl on his bitch. She said his girl goes to the same nail salon on the same day every week," True responded.

"I need somebody on that bitch ASAP! I don't need her to disappear for shit. You know how bitches can be, so make sure whoever you got following her ass don't fuck this up otherwise she's dead." Bread said.

"Bet that. I already let 'ol girl know that we don't play that shit. She knows that we get rid of bloodlines. Our reputation proceeds us, bro."

"Good shit then. As soon as she spots that bitch Dee, I need a call."

We went on to discuss other business because even though all our families were under attack, business had to go on. Since both Bread and I had our traps hit, that made Butta shut shit down on his end for a while. He was only taking calls for pounds or better. So were we. I still had no clue what them niggas working with Deuce looked like, so we all had to be on our P's and Q's. We wrapped shit up and headed back to the room.

Storm said goodbye to everybody, and so did I. This was more than enough for one day for my baby. I needed to get her home, so she could relax. We left and got in the car. I headed towards the house we had out West, but tomorrow, she was going to Romeoville until shit got squared away. We arrived fifty minutes later, took a shower and went slam to sleep. Holding Storm always put me to sleep. That was one of the first days I slept good in a long ass time.

The next morning, Storm was up before me. I

smelled bacon and eggs, and my stomach growled. I got up, pissed and washed my hands before heading downstairs. I walked into the kitchen and saw Storm bent over taking biscuits out the oven. Her ass was sitting up real nice. All she had on was a t-shirt and panties. It was the sexiest thing I've ever seen. I walked up and wrapped my arms around her. I kissed her on her neck, and she giggled.

I smacked her on the ass and went to the table. Even when she's all fucked up, my baby still wanted to take care of me. She made my plate and set it in front of me. She turned back around to get my glass of orange juice and her plate. She sat my cup and her plate down. She went back to get her juice and sat down across the table from me. We said grace and dug in.

"So bae, I need you to go to the house out in Romeoville until further notice."

"Why, bae? I like being in the city." Storm whined.

"Being in the city got you put in the hospital. Being in the city can make me kill people's families. That ain't a good look bae. Please, just listen to me this time. Go to the Romeoville house."

"I guess, Halo," Storm said rolling her eyes.

"Ain't no I guess, woman. Just do the shit. As soon as everything is done and over with, we can go wherever you wanna go, I promise."

"Pinky promise?" Storm asked holding out her pinky.

"Pinky promise, bae. I'll be leaving here within the next two hours, so I need you to leave when I do that way I won't have to worry about you."

"Ok man, damn. What about all my stuff?"

"I never said we weren't coming back, bae, just leaving here for a 'lil bit."

"A'ight."

Storm didn't even finish her breakfast. She stomped up the stairs to do who knows what. I'll be damned if I didn't finish my breakfast first. I was hungry as fuck. As soon as I finished, I washed my plate and fork and placed them in the strainer. I headed upstairs so I could pacify my big ass baby. When I walked into the bedroom clothes were thrown everywhere, and it looked like her entire shoe collection was on our bed. I walked over there and picked up a pair of blood red Louboutins.

"Storm, bring that ass here, girl!" I yelled.

"What, Halo? I'm trying to pack."

"Fuck that shit. You actin' like you need some act right, so I'ma give it to you. Take that shit off and put these on ONLY these."

Storm smirked at me as she took off her clothes. She slid her feet into the heels and bent over in front of me giving me a perfect look at her pussy. That thang was juicy and dripping. I dropped to my knees behind her and smacked her ass. I slid my tongue up her pussy all the way to her ass. She let out a low hiss. I slurped her pussy like I was thirsty, and she quenched my thirst. I played with her clit while I slurped and licked her up.

I felt her start to shake, so I wrapped my arms around her waist. She bucked back fucking my face, and I loved that shit. I felt her reach back and grab my dreads. It was on now. I went in on her ass, and she squirted, but I kept going. Damn, her pussy tasted so fucking good. When she busted for a second time, I left her alone. She laid down on the floor with her ass in the air. That was perfect because that's how I wanted her.

I dropped my pants and stepped out of them. I dropped to my knees again and positioned myself behind her. She pushed her ass back against me, but I pulled back. I wanted to tease the fuck outta her. I wanted her to beg for it. I wanted to hear her moan. All that shit was so sexy to me.

"Halo, stoooooopppppppp! Give it to me, bae."

"Nah, you actin' up, bae. I don't think I should give you anything."

"Please bae, please. I promise to be a good girl."

"You say that, but once I give you what you want, you gon' act the same."

"I promise I wo-"

I cut Storm off from talking when I rammed into her. She yelled out, and I started to pummel her pussy. She had that ass arched up just like I loved it. I grabbed the back of her neck and fucked her silly. She was screaming and hollering. I dug deep in her shit. I wanted her to know I meant business. I leaned forward to whisper in her ear.

"You gon' do what I said?"

"Yes bae, yasssssss. Damn, this shit feels so good."

"You goin' to the Romeoville house, right?"

"Yasssss. Oh, my God! Right there, bae, I'm cummmmiiiiinnnngggggg!"

Storm squirted all over me just as I came too. I slapped her one more time on the ass before I got up. I went into the bathroom and went straight to the shower while she composed herself. I knew she'd come in the shower when she finally got up. No sooner did I think it then she came into the shower. I was one of those people who really didn't like head but loved giving it. I liked the shit every now and then though, and it was like Storm knew it too.

She got down on her knees and played with me. Once I was good and ready, she put her mouth on me. I threw my head back as I grabbed her dreads. She was doing that shit just right, and I knew I was about to cum. Just a few minutes later, I came all in her mouth, and she kept going. My bitch was the truth. When I finished, Storm stood up and kissed me deeply. I slid my tongue in her mouth and sucked her tongue and lips. I washed her then she washed me before we got out.

Storm got dressed in an all-pink Nike sweat suit, and I matched her swag in all-black. I kissed my woman, gave her some money, and we both grabbed our things before leaving. Storm got into her white-on-white Mercedes CLK, and I slid into my Nissan Armada. I needed my big boy car for the big boy shit I was on. She blew me a kiss as we both turned out the driveway. She went right, and I went left.

Something felt off, but I shook it off. I knew that my girl was on her way to safety. Beauty and the kids were still in the hospital and Bread had that shit covered. Butta wouldn't even let Baby go anywhere with security. We had all angles covered, but I still couldn't shake the feeling that something was off. All a muhfucka could do was pray that everything was good.

Chapter Thirteen

Storm

I jumped on I-290 to head out like Halo wanted me to. After I got sexed like I did, damn right I was going to listen to bae. I was good until I hit the interchange. That's when I realized I forgot my phone. I got off and turned around to go back to the house. I made it back in record time and parked on the street. I planned to be in and out in five minutes tops. I unlocked the door and left it that way as I closed it. I remember leaving my phone on the dresser.

I ran upstairs to grab my shit and leave. I headed straight to the bedroom and scooped my phone up. I was in and out with no problems. I locked the door and hopped back into my whip. Just as I cranked my car up, I called Halo, so I could let bae know I had to go back for my phone. Halo didn't answer the phone, so I left a message. I drove back towards the e-way and got on. Just as I hit the interchange, my phone rang. I saw that it was Halo, so I answered.

"Hey bae, I just wanted you to know that I left my

phone at the house, so I went back to get it."

"Ok, smooth. You headed back out though, right?"

"Yeah, I'm near the interchange now. I love you and see you when you get ho-"

I was interrupted when a gun was jammed in my side. I heard Halo yelling into the phone, but I couldn't do shit.

"Hand me the fucking phone, bitch."

I did as I was told.

"Halo baby, how you feelin'?" I heard the nigga say into the phone.

I knew Halo was throwing a fit, but I couldn't hear what was being said.

"You love your bitch or nah?" He paused. "You know, you ain't in the position to be making demands right now. Maybe your bitch can do a better job at saving her own life."

I breathed in deeply thinking about what I could do. This nigga had his gun jammed dead into my rib cage. I already knew that no matter what I did, it would result in me getting killed, or at the very least, getting hurt. He passed me the phone back, and I damn near cried.

"Bae, just do whatever that nigga says. I swear I'ma get you outta this shit. On my life, I got you, bae. Just trust me."

"I trust you, bae. I love you," I said back.

"Wrong move, bitch."

I heard a loud blast, and then I lost control of my car. I screamed from both the bullet that seared through my stomach and my car spinning out. I remember crashing into the median. As I struggled to breathe, I heard the back door open. Out my peripheral and to my left, I saw someone walk to the driver side window. A gun was shoved in my broken window. I saw the barrel and started praying. I didn't pray for forgiveness or no shit like that. I prayed that Halo found this nigga and killed his entire family.

Shot after shot pumped into my body, and I felt each one. I heard a click and yelled out Halo's name. After that, I succumbed to the darkness that enveloped my body. I tried to hold on as long as I could, but it got cold. All I could think of was Halo. *Bae, I love you.*

Chapter Fourteen

Halo

I was trippin'. I had to be to get the call I just got. Storm just called me saying she had to double back to get her phone. I told shorty that I loved her, and I would do whatever I needed to do to get her right. As soon as she said she'd see me at home, she got cut off. The nigga who took the phone was on straight bullshit. I was mad as fuck, but there was really nothing I could do, so I told Storm to do whatever he said. I heard a blast and a lot of screaming. I felt helpless as fuck because somebody was at my girl, and I couldn't do shit.

I had to sit on the phone and listen as my girl was gunned the fuck down. I heard a crash and then more blasting. I screamed into the phone and knew there was nothing I could do. All I knew was that she was on the interchange headed South. I ran to my car and hopped in. I gunned it towards the e-way never explaining to Bread, Butta, or True what was going on.

They were all blowing up my phone, but I didn't answer. I just kept screaming for Storm to say something to me. I was hurt like a bitch. I strained to hear my girl despite all the noise.

"Bae, bae…" Storm coughed. "Get that nigga. Love you."

'Storm, bae!" I screamed. "Bae, please hold on for me. I'm calling the police and shit now. Hold on for me. HOLD ON FOR ME!" I screamed into my phone.

The phone hung up, and I couldn't do shit but cry. While Storm was on one end, I called the police on my burner phone. I told them that she was at the I-290 and I-90/94 Interchange. I screamed at their asses to hurry up and get there as I heard my girl get shot over and over again. Talk about a muthafucka's heart hurting. I didn't know what to expect when I got to the interchange, but I didn't expect what I found. I pulled up and hopped out.

My girl was in the front seat of her car with a ton of bullet holes in her. Fuck ass CPD didn't even have the decency to cover her up. I ran up and got stopped. I didn't even give a fuck that I swung on a cop. That was my fucking girl! Once they figured out who I was, they let me through. I knelt down next to Storm's car door and cried heavily. My baby was gone. Her blood leaked down across the seat and out the door. Her face was untouched, but I couldn't say the same for her body. I was so fucked up.

I remember being asked a shit load of questions. I remember being in shock. I remember my baby's last words. Come hell or high water, I'd honor that shit. Whoever the fuck did this, and my money was on Deuce, they were gonna die.

***

The next few hours were a blur. I was approached by cop after cop and asked question after question. Shit was redundant. All I wanted to do was be with my girl, my soon-to-be wife, my everything. Storm was who I lived for. What the fuck was I 'posed to do now? Now I had to plan a damn funeral. I didn't wanna fuck with nothing and nobody. The detective assigned to Storm's case gave me his card and left after not getting any answers from me. He wouldn't get shit anyway.

I sat in that hospital room while my girl laid on the bed, dead. I ain't never cried like this before. Storm was one of the first people to love and understand me besides my pops. She was my lifeline. Every move I made, I made with her in mind. My heart was hurting like fucking crazy. I didn't know what I'd do now. My world was gone. Whoever did this shit was gon' die and so would their family.

Four hours later, the nurse came to tell me that the coroner was there for Storm. I didn't want to let go. I couldn't let go. How the hell was I supposed to let go of the woman I loved? There was no way in hell. I stood next to her bedside holding her hand. She had long since went cold, but I didn't care. I professed my love to her. I told her that I would've given my life for hers if I could. I swear, I would trade my life for hers. Dead ass.

The coroner took her away from me, staring at me with sad eyes. I didn't know what to do. I hadn't even called anybody back yet. When I finally got some peace and quiet, I hit up True. I told him what all happened and to call Bread and Butta. Shit had gotten outta hand big time. I already knew that one of the lil' goons Deuce was dealing with had something to do with this. All I had to do was prove it.

Five days went by, and all I could do was cry. My nigga True took care of all the funeral arrangements. He was the real MVP. I just couldn't do it. Once the reality of it all set in on me, I lost my shit. I spazzed the fuck out. My girl was dead. A fuck nigga killed her, and I didn't even know who did the shit. All we knew is that Deuce had something to do with the shit.

Walking into the church, everything was a blur. Tears fell heavily down my eyes, and although my eyes were covered with my signature Gucci shades, everyone saw them. The thing was, I didn't give a fuck. My everything was laying in that casket at the end of the aisle, and I didn't know if I could face her.

I failed her. I should've protected her. I should've been there to make sure nothing happened to her. When the word came to me, it rocked me to my knees. Nothing my niggas could say or do could ever take away the pain I felt. For that shit, niggas had to die. I was running up in houses and killing whole muthafuckin' bloodlines behind this shit right here. My girl, my wife? Niggas touched her, so they had to pay. There was no way I was about to just sit back and let this shit go.

I struggled to get down to the front of the aisle. Each step got harder and harder. I felt like my Louboutins had cement on the bottom of them. I finally stood in front of the casket, and I broke the fuck down. Storm looked so fuckin' beautiful. I leaned over to kiss her and damn near passed out. I needed my girl. I clung to the edge of her casket flanked by all my day one niggas. True reached out to me and touched my shoulder. I turned to look at him, and he gave me a slight head nod. I straightened up and looked to where he motioned to. My blood began to boil.

"Fuck is you doin' here, bruh? You think shit is a game?"

"Nun like that, Halo. Just paying my respects."

"Fuck yo' respect. Pay me in blood, my nigga."

"Is a fight really what you want?"

"Fuck a fight. This shit is war!" I roared.

I watched as Deuce walked out with his weak ass entourage. That nigga always thought he had one up on a nigga, but tonight, he'd find out different. I wasn't about to play with nobody. I don't know why niggas always wanted to test my gangsta. I turned back around to my girl when True leaned into me to speak. This nigga knew just what to say.

"We doin' that tonight?"

"And you know it. Nobody sleeps, eats, or breathes the right way after tonight. Whole bloodlines, my nigga. Start with his mama."

"Bet that."

Chapter Fifteen

True

I already knew how Halo was feeling. When my girl was killed, I wanted to kill everybody. Kalila meant everything to me, so I know how Halo felt. When Deuce's bitch ass showed up, he tried to play like shit was cool, but we knew what it was. This had his name written all over it. Either way, it goes, he was a dead man. Deuce was gonna die behind this shit here.

I knew where his mama stayed at. He tried telling people that his mama been dead, but we knew better. His grandma was even still alive. She had to go along with his mother and his girl. If we had to, we'd kill his girl's people too. No fucks were given right now. I had to watch my best friend do the same shit I did a few years ago, so I felt Halo's pain. There was no getting out of this.

Once Halo was at the crib for the repast, I decided to stay out. I had my own lil' squad of hittas. We went out riding for Deuce. We didn't get his ass that night, but both his mama and grandma were left unguarded. I didn't give not one fuck. I bodied both them hoes before setting the house on fire. He should know by morning that his people were gone if not sooner. I headed back to the house to check on Halo. I already knew my friend wasn't no good. When I walked in, I could see that Halo had lost it.

"My fuckin' girl is gone! Niggas wanna try me. Shit is real out here. Fuck that nigga! Whole fuckin' bloodlines my nigga, whole bloodlines!" Halo yelled.

This was my best friend, and I felt Halo's pain. I knew how this shit went. Halo was gonna get worse before getting better. When you lose your other half, shit is hard to get back right. It was gonna be a long ass time before Halo would be straight and as the best friend, it was my job to make sure my friend was all good. I took Halo in another room to calm down. I had Bread and Butta watching shit like a hawk. Shit was bad, but it was about to get ten times worse.

***

Once I finally got Halo to sit down somewhere, I cleared the house out. It was just The Faction in the house minus Deuce. We had to come up with a way to flush his ass out. While I was sitting there thinking, my phone rang. I checked my phone to see it was 'ol girl. I hurried to pick it up.

"What's good?"

"I see Deuce's girl right now. I'm in the mall. What should I do?"

"What mall you in?"

"Ford City."

"Bet that. Go find a way to talk to her or some shit and keep her occupied until I can get there."

"A'ight. I'm getting paid for this shit, right?"

"Damn girl, yeah. Do what the fuck I said. One more thing."

"What?"

"Go park your car in the farthest corner of the parking lot and make sure it's dark."

"Ok."

I hung up the phone and saw everybody looking at me. I relayed to them what the phone call was about, and Halo jumped up quick. I already knew the shit Halo was on, so I didn't even stop it. I felt like me and

Halo could handle everything, so we let the twins go to be with their families. I told Butta that I'd hit his line if we needed them. We dapped them up, and they left. Bread was still on edge anyway because Beauty was still in a coma. For safety reasons, Butta had Baby stay at the hospital with the security we hired for them.

They left, and we suited up. As we put on our bulletproof vests and checked our guns, I thought about what might be going through Halo's mind. I knew how I felt when Kalila was killed, but I didn't have to hear the shit when it went down. Storm was on the phone with Halo when everything went down. I knew that had to be fucking with my homie's mental.

"Yo, you good Halo? If you're not ready for this shit, then I can handle it. I'll cut you in on everything because I know what it feels like to want revenge."

"I'm straight," Halo said with no emotion.

"That bitch is as good as dead. I want Deuce to feel every bit of my pain. Our pain. I don't just want his ass dead, I wanna torture his ass. I want him to know that death is imminent for him. Before he dies, I want his ass to see my face."

MARINA J

"Bet that. 'Ol girl just texted me saying that she sitting with Dee in the food court. How you wanna do this shit? Go in guns blazing or have her bring Dee to us?"

"The less people in my way, the better. Have her bring Dee out the mall and to us."

We didn't say another word. We left the house and headed towards a warehouse we had. There we had a few different cars we used to go make plays. I knew that either one of us could use our cars. For this, we had to be incognito. We made it there and chose an old Ford Taurus. We left and headed South towards Ford City Mall. The e-way was clear, so we got there in no time and parked all the way in the back of the parking lot. Good thing for us, the lights were broken, and there were no signs of cameras.

I hit 'ol girl up and told her to bring her out. A few minutes later we saw them walking in our direction. Thankfully, 'ol girl listened when I told her to park her car in the back of the lot too. The closer they got, the easier it was to hear them. They were babbling on and on about some shit that women talk about. I didn't give no fucks. We were parked a few cars over just watching and waiting. As soon as they rounded the back of the car and the trunk went up, that was our cue.

We slid out the car, guns ready to go and crept over to them. When I tell you that 'ol girl performed for an award, shorty did that. She screamed and was crying too. When I hit her and told her to shut the fuck up, she fell to the ground and curled up in a fetal position. I was gone dick her down real good for this shit here. Halo grabbed Dee by her throat, and that's when the recognition of who we were set in.

"H-h-halo, I swear I didn't have nothing to do with this shit. It was all Deuce."

"Where the fuck is the loyalty? Even though you gone tell me what I wanna know, I woulda thought you woulda held out a little longer. These hoes ain't loyal."

Halo dragged Dee back to our car and got in the back seat with her. I saw the car rocking back and forth as Halo beat the shit outta Dee. Fuck that bitch though. She had it coming. I picked 'ol girl up off the ground and made sure she was straight. She pushed me and went to hit me when I grabbed her wrist.

"Damn nigga, you ain't have to hit me." She hissed.

"I had to make shit look real shorty. Damn, what is your real name?" I asked confused.

"You been fucking me for months now and you don't remember my name? The fuck kinda shit is that? You spend months with a nigga and done had his dick in ya throat more times than I can count, and you can't remember my name? That shit is so disrespectful."

"My bad a'ight. Just tell me again, and I promise I won't forget it."

"Honesty."

"Well damn, check you out. Honesty and True sounds good together, don't it?"

As she nodded her head, I saw a sparkle in her eyes. Sure enough, I had been fucking with her longer than any other chick I smashed, but I didn't know about making her mine. She was about her money, so I'll give her that, but I've never had to give her money before nor did she come at me on some pay my bills type shit either. Maybe Honesty could be my new chick. I'd have to think about that another time. I pecked her on the lips making her the first chick I ever kissed besides Kalila and sent her on her way.

I made my way back to the car and Halo was still beating on Dee. Her ass was unconscious, but that didn't stop Halo. I had to grab Halo and tell the homie to chill out. We rode out back to the warehouse, so we could do what we do. Cruising down the e-way, a ton of shit crossed my mind. Snatching Dee up was too easy. It was like Deuce wasn't even protecting her. Maybe he wanted us to snatch his bitch or maybe he didn't even care. I kinda felt like Deuce wouldn't give a fuck either way. When we pulled into the warehouse, Halo grabbed Dee and pulled her limp body inside by her legs not giving a fuck about anything else. She woke up screaming, but all that did was piss Halo off again. Halo kicked her hard as fuck in her stomach, and that shut her up.

Halo picked Dee up and pushed her into a chair. Meticulously tying her up, Halo made sure that the rope was tight, and Dee couldn't get out. She looked at us with a bloody face crying. She was begging and pleading, but that shit fell on deaf ears. Halo was long gone, and the person bro was now was nothing like my friend used to be. I stepped back and let Halo handle business. I needed Dee to talk before Halo killed her, so I stepped in every now and then. By the time we were done, Dee had spilled everything.

Chapter Sixteen

Deuce

I knew I wasn't playing fair, but I didn't give a fuck. This was my muthafuckin' city! If I had to lay down The Faction in order to be king, then I'd do that shit. The one thing I noticed about Halo and them, was that they all loved their bitches. I knew that would be the best way to make their asses weak. I started by having my lil' niggas beat the shit outta Storm, but that didn't work. Halo was still in the streets making moves. Then I had them fuck with Beauty, but all that did was cause Bread to hire security and some more shit. They couldn't even finish the job.

As soon as Butta found out about his sister-in-law, he put Baby on the same type of lockdown that Bread had his family on. I needed all these niggas gone like yesterday. True didn't have a bitch, so I wasn't too much worried about his ass. He was just Halo's do-boy. Every time Halo told his punk ass to jump, he did that shit. It did nothing but irritate me because True worshipped the ground that Halo walked on. I bet if he knew Halo's lil' secret that they wouldn't be friends anymore.

Now, these niggas had killed my mama and my grandmama. I'd been spitting a story about them being dead for the longest time just so no niggas wouldn't be all in my shit. I knew how they all got down. That was some shit all our pops' had laid down. Whole fuckin' bloodlines. That way there was no retaliation from anyone in a person's family should we have to get rid of their asses. Eliminate the entire threat. That shit had been drilled into us as kids, so I already knew what it was.

Not only did they kill the only people I cared about but they burned the house down too. I had to avenge my girls. I wasn't worried about Dee's ass. That sounds like some heartless ass shit, right? Truth was, it was her snake ass that put the idea in my head. I met her a year and a half ago. I did love her at first, but after finding out that the only reason she got at me was because True had hurt her feelings, I stopped giving a fuck about her.

Apparently, one of my lil' niggas, Drop, told me that Dee used to get piped down by True. I ain't never care about True or any of the bitches he fucked with, so I never made it a point to go behind a nigga and find out his business. When Dee first put the idea in my head that I should be running shit, I agreed with her. She even went so far as to help me come up with a team of niggas who would help me get rid of everybody else. All I had to do was promise them a spot on my team after I was running shit. If they were thorough, then they'd have a spot.

As time went on, Dee really started pressing the issue of me moving on The Faction not knowing that it had to be a slow process, so people wouldn't put two and two together that fast. It was like she didn't care, so that's when I started snooping and Drop brought me the bullshit. Dee didn't get security or anything. If them niggas snatched her ass up, then so be it. By the time she told them anything, I would be long gone, and they wouldn't be able to find me unless I wanted them too.

I showed my face at Storm's funeral after I had Core take care of her ass. It was time to shake the muthafuckin' table. I wanted Halo and the rest of their asses to know that anybody could get touched at any time. I didn't care that they knew it was me who had shit jumping off. When it was all said and done, I'd be the last one standing and the city would be mine. I wanted to make Halo my bitch and that all started with getting rid of Storm. You make the head weak, and the body follows suit. Them niggas looked at Halo like some sort of God. I wanted to fuck that image up. My phone rang bringing me out of my thoughts.

"Yo!"

"Niggas grabbed Dee up from the mall. For a smart bitch she dumb as hell. I don't see how she didn't read that play as grimy as she is."

"Fuck allat. Who grabbed her?"

"Halo and True."

"Bet that. You got them on the radar?"

"I got Bose and Zane following them now. They took her to some old ass warehouse. What you want us to do?"

"Just sit tight for right now. Don't make a move until I say so."

"A'ight."

I hung up and paced the room. I was hiding out in a condo downtown that nobody knew about. In order for the rest of this shit to go off like I wanted to, I had to stay hidden for the time being. Me popping up at Storm's funeral was just the beginning. I needed all them niggas on edge. If I got lucky, I could catch all their asses in one place and get rid of them all at one time. That was wishful thinking though. But, I knew for a fact that I'd be able to catch Halo and True together. Even if I couldn't get at anybody else, I wanted Halo's ass bad. I was gonna show that muthafucka who was in charge.

From the outside looking in, niggas would think I had a hard-on for Halo, and I did but not in that way. Growing up it was always Halo this or Halo that. Even my own pops used to try to compare me to Halo. I got tired of that dumb shit. It was like my pops wished Halo was his kid instead of me. You know what that will do to a kid who looks up to their pops? I was jealous as fuck. What was so much better about Halo that my own father wanted me to be like that muthafucka?

Pops sang Halo's praises because Halo always did shit better than me. We both went everywhere with our fathers. We were bred for this shit. This wasn't just a lifestyle for us. This was really our life, and my pops favored Halo over me. That's why when he died I didn't give a fuck. That's why Halo had to fucking go. Wasn't no way in hell that I was about to be walking around taking orders from Halo's bitch ass. Na uh, not this nigga here. Come hell or high water, Halo was gonna die, and that was my word.

***

Drop hit me back letting me know that Halo and True still had Dee in the warehouse. Bose and Zane wanted a break, so he was sending Kilo and Core to take their place. That was fine by me. As long as I had eyes on those niggas, then I could make my next move. Once Drop confirmed that the guys had switched I gave him another job. He was going down to Northwestern to check some shit out for me. I needed eyes on the twins. Since they were on Halo's side, I needed them gone too.

I got lucky when Bread's bitch got hit by a truck. I was just planning to have Drop scare the fuck outta her, but she did that shit to herself. I heard that one of the kids had died. That meant that Bread was about to hold a funeral too. Shit just kept getting better and better for me. Drop sent me a text and let me know that he made it to the hospital. I told him to keep his eyes and ears open and let me know everything he found out.

While I waited for something to happen, I rolled a blunt and sat down. I cut the tv on and tried to find a game to watch. I honestly needed some pussy and some fye ass head. I called up this one lil' chick I been fucking with and told her to come through. She was a get money type of broad. I kept her on reserve ever since I found out about Dee's trifling ass. At least with this chick, I knew what shit was. She let me know she was on the way, so I hung up.

I knew I had at least an hour before she got there, so I finished my blunt and went to go wash my nuts. Since she was coming ready for it, I figured I could have clean balls for her. I laughed to myself because that was the least of my worries right now but whatever. As soon as I threw on my Jordan basketball shorts the doorbell rang. I buzzed her and waited for her to come upstairs. I stayed on the ninth floor so I knew it would take a few minutes to get up here. My dick was already ready because I knew I was about to get some good shit.

I heard a knock, so I opened the door. I swear shorty was the shit. She was on it because all she had on was a jacket that stopped at her knees. On her feet were some purple Louboutin pumps. Shit was mad sexy. She walked in, and as soon as I closed the door, she dropped her coat. Underneath she had on a thong and bra that matched her pumps. Shorty was sexy as fuck; on God.

I pulled her lil' chocolate ass to me and tongued her down. She slid her tongue in my mouth and swirled that shit around. My dick got harder and was poking her short ass in the stomach. She pushed away from me and dropped to her knees. She wasted no time slurping my dick up between her plump lips. Shorty went to work on my ass, and I had to back up to the wall. She never missed a beat and moved with me. Yes, Lawd!

"Got damn, girl. Suck this dick. Get it sloppy just like daddy likes it. Damn, Honesty. FUCK!"

I felt my nut coming, and I swear I saw a white light. I came hard as fuck, and she swallowed all of that shit. Shorty was the real MVP. Super Head ain't have shit on her. I pulled her up and pushed her towards the couch. I bent her over the arm of the couch and grabbed a magnum. I rolled it down my stiff dick and plunged into. Ooooh weeee, she was tight as fuck! I pumped into her, slowly at first gripping her hips. Honesty screamed out in pleasure and hearing her moan turned me on to the fullest.

I slapped her ass and watched it jiggle as I hit it from the back hard. I felt my nut getting ready to come, so I pulled out. I told her to lay on the couch so I could hit it like that. I didn't wanna nut yet, so I was gonna hit her this way. I wanted to savor this feeling because her pussy was too good. I hit her missionary for a cool twenty minutes before we switched positions again. I sat down and made her ride my shit.

Why the fuck did I do that? Shorty's pussy hugged my dick like a glove as she slid down on me. Honesty bounced up and down like she had a point to prove. Before I knew it, my nut was rising the fuck up and I couldn't stop her ass if I wanted to. I came hard as shit and grabbed shorty to me. If she played her cards right, she could be my queen when I became king of the city. I sat there for a minute as I came down off my high before letting her climb off my lap.

She headed to the bathroom to clean herself up. I sat there asshole naked with the condom still on. I dead ass couldn't feel my legs. Honesty had my ass fucked up. When she came back out the bathroom, she started putting her shit back on. I grabbed my shorts and pulled a knot of money out my pocket. I passed it to her, and she planted a kiss on my lips before leaving. Now a nigga could go to sleep in peace. Hopefully, I'd be able to get a few hours of sleep before Drop called me.

I flushed the condom and cleaned my dick off in the sink. I put my shorts back on and made sure the door was locked before I went to my bedroom. I needed sleep like yesterday, but with everything going on, I hadn't been to sleep in almost forty-eight hours. I climbed into my bed and passed out with my phone in my hand. I don't even remember falling asleep, but I do remember when my phone rang. It was Drop so I answered it quick.

"Yo boss, you need to make a move."

"Fuck you mean? Them niggas moving or what?" I asked.

"Yeah, they headed your way. That lil, bitch that left from over there fuck with them, niggas. She just sent 'em to you."

"Good looking. I'll call you in a few."

FUCK! How the fuck I didn't read that play? I grabbed a few things before stuffing my phone in my pocket and snatching my keys off the nightstand. I took off out the door not giving a fuck if it was locked or not. I hit the stairs and ran down them to the garage. I pulled the door open and took off to my car. I was driving an all-black Challenger. It wasn't my main car, and that's how I was able to keep under the radar from them niggas. I whipped out the parking spot and sped out the garage. I made a left turn coming out the garage. Thank God for tinted windows because I saw True rolling in with another nigga in the car with him.

I had to refrain from rolling the window down and shooting his ass. Soon though. Pretty soon I'd be able to do to his ass what I wanted to. Halo and the rest of them niggas too. They got me good this time, but I would get them back even better.

Chapter Seventeen

True

When Honesty hit my jack, I knew she made good on her promise. She said she could help me find Deuce, and I was with that shit. Right now, I was on straight bullshit. I rode out with one of my young hittas headed to the condo Honesty told me about. It took no time for us to get there. We parked and hopped out taking the stairs. I had the lil' homie go ahead of me because if Deuce saw me, he knew what it was already.

He motioned for me to come out the stairwell, so I did. I crept to the door with my gun out. We saw that the door was cracked, so that meant one of two things: either he was tipped off, and he left, or somebody got his ass before we did. We stormed inside and checked every single room. The nigga had definitely been there, but he wasn't there now. That means somebody dropped his ass a line. I was pissed the fuck off. I checked around to see if his dumb ass left anything that might've told me where he was going. I ain't find shit, and that pissed me off even further.

I shot Honesty a text and let her know that we got found out. I wanted her to stay away from Deuce in the meantime. I already knew that if he got a hold of her, he'd kill her, and I didn't want that for her. She was the first woman besides Kalila that made me feel something. I didn't even care what she had to do with this nigga tonight. The fact that she was down to help me with both Deuce and his bitch let me know she was thorough and about her shit. Shorty was genuine from what I could see.

We left mad as fuck. I headed back to my spot after dropping my young hitta off. I called Honesty and told her to come over. She got there within an hour. When I opened the door, she had her head down. I lifted her chin so she'd look at me. Tears flooded her eyes, and that shit did something to me. I pulled her to me and kissed her deeply. I slammed the door and locked it behind her. I grabbed her hand and led her to my bedroom.

I proceeded to undress her slowly. She cried the entire time. I kissed every tear that fell. I laid her down on the bed and did the one thing I swore I wouldn't do since Kalila died: I slid in her without a condom. This shit was just as heavy for me as it was for her. I slow stroked the fuck outta Honesty as she gripped me close to her. I made love to that woman. The only thing about it was that I felt like I was cheating on Kalila because she was the only woman I had ever made love to.

The shit was so good, and I ain't gon' lie, I nutted fast. I wasn't even in the pussy a good thirty minutes before I was cumming. Honesty was still crying as I finished and pulled her to me. I fell asleep with her in my arms. Today was a fucked-up day, but shorty proved to me that she was down to ride. I couldn't really let her go after that, but I was stuck. Was I really cheating on Kalila when Kalila was dead? That's what the shit felt like. I prayed that Kalila would forgive me.

***

When I woke up, I was in bed by myself. I don't know where Honesty went, but from the smell in the air, she was in my kitchen. I took a piss and brushed my teeth. I walked out my room and into the kitchen to see Honesty making breakfast. I sat down at the table and waited until shorty was finished. She made my plate, grabbed the juice, and brought it to the table. I had cheese eggs, grits, French toast, sausage, bacon, and biscuits. I was about to smash the fuck outta this food. Kalila was the only other woman who ever cooked for me. Otherwise, I ate out unless Halo, Bread, or Butta invited me to the crib 'cuz their women cooked. Honesty was the shit right now.

I smashed my plate and sat back full. Honesty looked at me with fear in her eyes, and I knew I had to pacify her. I told her to come sit on my lap, and she did. She looked at me with so much worry in her eyes. Everything in me was screaming to save her, but my head was stopping me. Kalila was my heart. Was I ready to move on to the next woman? I had to really think about that, but I knew I felt something for Honesty.

I put my dishes in the sink and led Honesty back to the room. I undressed her without a word and led her into the bathroom. We showered together, and I caressed every inch of her as I washed her body. Shorty was shaking and everything. I didn't even stick dick to her either. I just washed her body then rinsed her off. I stepped out the shower and grabbed a towel to wrap her in. I led her into the room and pulled the blanket back. She caught the hint and laid down.

I kissed her on the forehead and told her I'd be back. I needed to go clear my head for a minute. Since Kalila died, I didn't get attached to these females out here. I just gave 'em dick, and that was it. Honesty had me feeling a different type of way. I knew that what I asked her to do for me when it came to Deuce and Dee was some heavy shit. Normally, I'd just toss cash at a bitch and go about my business, but shorty was showing me something different. I knew I felt something for her when I ran up in her raw. I didn't even care about the consequences.

I got in my car and decided to hit Lake Shore Drive. A drive near the lakefront always cleared my head. We were about to be in some heavy shit these next few days. There was no telling what might happen. Tomorrow was never promised to anybody.

All I could think about though was if something happened to me, what about Honesty? That's how I knew I cared for her more than I should have. Shit was crazy.

I drove around for about two hours before Halo hit my line. I picked up and heard some shouting and some more shit. I didn't know what the fuck was going on, but I sped towards the warehouse because that's where I left Halo when I got the call about Deuce. I hoped like hell nothing was wrong with Halo. I don't think I could deal with any more bad news. Shit, Beauty still hadn't woken up yet. Bread was all fucked up about it.

We knew that Deuce was on good bullshit, so he had his daughter cremated instead of having a funeral. We didn't need Deuce trying to show up and cause more chaos. Nah, we needed him to get comfortable. I turned into the warehouse parking lot and hopped out barely putting my shit in park. I ran inside and saw Halo covered in blood. What remained of Dee sat in the chair she was tied to. Halo was screaming, crying and a bloody fucking mess.

"Yo Halo, you good, bro?"

"Am I good? Bruh, I'm fucked up! My girl is gone, and this ignorant bitch had everything to do with it because of you!" Halo shouted.

"What you mean because of me? I ain't even know the hoe!"

"After you left, the bitch kept talking. She said you used to stick dick to her, but you tossed her ass to the side like she was nothing. Said that she ended up fucking with Deuce on some revenge type shit and that she'd do whatever she could to try to get at you. She was watching Storm, Beauty, and Baby. After a while, she wanted Deuce to get rid of all of us, and then she'd be queen next to his bum ass. Fuck you, my nigga!"

"What the fuck? How you blamin' me for some shit? How the fuck was I 'posed to know a bitch would get crazy over some dick? You can't blame the shit that happened to the women on me. My girl was killed too, but you forget about that shit, right? A nigga been grievin', so don't come at me with that bullshit."

"Fuck you mean? Nigga, Kalila been dead how long now? Fuck outta here! You still using that same shit. You out here sticking dick to bitches but not remembering faces? You all the way wrong. Like right now, I feel like I should put a bullet in ya' ass, but you been my brother since forever. That's the only thing saving you right now. From now on, I want you out of every fucking thing. You. Are. Done."

"How I'm done? I got your back, Halo. Out of every fucking thing, you really think I'd jeopardize what we been doin'? We been friends for way too long for shit to go down like this."

"I said what the fuck I said. Get ghost, my nigga."

I didn't even know what the fuck to say. My dog, my nigga, my bro, my best friend blamed me for his girl dying. How in the fuck did we get here? Dee was a conniving ass bitch. I don't even remember giving her any dick, to be honest. It was always fuck 'em and on to the next one. Who the fuck orchestrates a whole damn plan because she got cut off from the dick? My mind was fucking blown. For now, I'd just chill, but I'd always have Halo's back. I just had to do it from the shadows now.

Chapter Eighteen

Halo

I was going fucking crazy. After Dee told us all the shit Deuce was trying to do, I wanted to tear the city up looking for his ass. True had somebody on him, so when he got the call about it, he jetted outta here. I was still here with this bitch, and I wanted her dead. With the last little bit of breath she could muster, she told me some more shit about my own friend. She ran down the whole thing to me about True. What I couldn't figure out is why True didn't tell me they used to get down. Did he fuck that many chicks since Kalila died that he really didn't remember her?

Dee was a straight up psycho. Who the fuck does all that? When she told me how she watched all our women and planned everything that happened with them with Deuce, I lost it. I literally tore her to pieces. I didn't even know that I had that much rage inside me. Blood was everywhere, and I dialed True's number not giving a fuck how I was feeling at the moment. I know I said some ignorant ass shit but so what. Part of this was his fault, and that's just how the fuck I felt. Wasn't no changing that shit.

I made a call to the small crew I kept for clean-up and bounced. They knew how to get in and what to do. I walked out to my car, bloody and all on straight bullshit. I was going looking for Deuce's ass. I didn't give a fuck about much of anything at that point. I got in the car and cranked it up. I swear Storm was looking out for me. When the radio came on K-Ci & JoJo's *All My Life* was blaring out the speakers. That was the song she said she wanted to dance to at our wedding.

Instead of doing some stupid shit, I headed to the house. I couldn't even call it home anymore since Storm was gone. It took me no time to get there. I dragged my feet walking up to the door and putting my key in the lock. I went inside, locked up and headed to the shower. I stripped out my clothes on the way up the stairs. Shit felt so cold in our bedroom. I could still smell all Storm's girly ass perfume everywhere. I fell to my knees and screamed.

The pain that was tearing through me felt like I had died myself. I hadn't even properly tried to grieve yet because I didn't want the shit to be real. My baby was really gone. I laid there naked as the day I was born and cried my eyes and heart out. I cried for the kisses I would never give Storm again. I cried for the house we'd never turn into a home again. I cried for all the memories I had of being able to hold her, hug her and telling her I loved her. I cried over the fact that I'd never see her carry my child. I just fucking cried.

I finally got up and took my ass in the shower. I let the water get scalding hot and got in. I cleaned off all the blood that was on me and stuck my head under the nozzle. My thoughts were running rampant. One minute I thought about Storm then the next it was on Deuce, and what I'd do to his ass, then it was back to Storm. God, I was going to miss my baby. Shit would never be the same for me. I would never love another woman like I loved her. She was my everything.

I stayed in the shower until the water ran cold. I turned off the water and got out. I didn't even bother with a towel. I walked into the bedroom and got my ass into the bed. I opened the drawer to my nightstand and pulled out a pack of blunts and a bag of weed. I rolled up with nothing on my mind other than getting higher than a muthafuckin' kite so I could just pass out. Shit had just gotten too stressful. I put fire to the tip and inhaled. I let the smoke sit in my lungs for a second before exhaling.

Before I knew it, the blunt was gone, and I still wasn't sleepy. I was hungry as fuck though. I got out the bed and went downstairs to the kitchen. I pulled the freezer door open and saw a few containers with food in them next to the hot pockets and frozen pizza. I grabbed one of them and saw a small post-it note on it. I read the note and almost fuckin' lost it. Even in death bae made sure I was straight. I read the note again.

Bae, I made this because I know your ass probably didn't even eat today. Warm it up in the microwave for ten minutes. I love you, and you better eat all of it.

I looked at the other six containers that were in the freezer. They all had similar notes on them. Fuck my life right now! Here I was trying my best to pretend like shit was all good but my girl was giving me a reminder that she was gone. I did what the note said and stuck the shit in the microwave for ten minutes. I was lost in thought and barely heard the beep of the microwave. The beep of the back door opening up didn't miss me though. I pulled open the drawer closest to me and grabbed the Glock that was in there.

"Muthafuckin' Halo. Well, look what we have here. Ain't you comfortable?" Deuce said.

"Fuck you, nigga! Fuck you want? You ready to die?" I spat.

"See, the way I look at it, you ain't in the position to be saying shit really. I literally caught you with ya ass out. Damn Halo, is shit that bad?" He laughed.

"Fuck you and what you talking 'bout. Like I fuckin' said, you ready to die?" I asked cocking my Glock back.

"When the fuck you gone learn that you can't play this game like I can? You playing with the big boys right now and we both know that you never really been able to do that."

"That ain't shit but noise you talking. I can run

with the best of them. Make a testament of the rest of them. Splatter a nigga like I never gave a fuck about 'em."

"Shit sounds good, don't it? But you and I both know you never been cut from the same cloth as me. You ain't shit, but a bitch and Ima show you what I do to bitches."

Deuce lunged at me, and I pulled the trigger. I missed his ass and took off towards the stairs. I got halfway up before he grabbed my ankle and yanked me back. I kicked him in the face with my other foot. He let me go, and I took off. I'll be damned if I die in my birthday suit. I ran towards my room where I knew I had two more guns and all my clothes. I slammed the door behind me locking it and pushing the dresser over in front of it. That would buy me some time.

I grabbed the first thing I saw in the closet after pulling my guns off the shelf. I struggled to get my feet into the sweatpants I grabbed. I tossed some J's on my feet, threw my shirt on and slipped a hoodie over my head. By this time Deuce was at the door trying to kick it in. I heard a soft hiss and knew that he had a gun with a silencer on it. Smart shit. I didn't give a fuck if the neighbors knew though. I ran over to the window and broke it out. I yelled for somebody, anybody, I really didn't give a fuck. I was just trying to buy some time. I knew the nigga would run if the police came.

I ducked in my closet while he was still trying to get in the room. The whole door splintered and he climbed over the dresser. He wasted no time running towards the bed, but I let off a barrage of bullets. If he was gonna kill me today, then he'd have to earn that shit. I wasn't about to just lay the fuck down and die. For a second I thought that I shot his ass, so I looked but he got me. He punched me dead in my face, and I was dazed.

I dropped my Glock, and my other guns lay near my feet. Deuce reached back and punched me again. My vision got blurry, and I spit blood at his ass. He laughed and punched me again. He punched me over and over and over again. I was so fucked up at that point that I couldn't even think. I even saw Storm motioning for me to come to her. I put my arms up like I was walking towards her and everything got dark. I don't even remember passing out.

Chapter Nineteen

Deuce

I knew if I bided my time that I'd catch Halo slipping. I'll give it to them niggas; they got me with Honesty. If I ever caught that hoe again, she was dead. Once I was sure that Halo was knocked the fuck out, I grabbed Halo's leg and dragged that muthafucka out the room after pushing the dresser out the way. I don't know what Halo was doing by shouting out the window and shit. We were in the fucking hood where people minded they own got damn business.

I dragged that muthafucka down the stairs not giving one single fuck. Halo was already knocked out, and I didn't care if it stayed that way until I got where I was going. I got to the front door and looked outside just in case a muthafucka decided to be bold today. Seeing that nobody was outside, I was all good. I tossed Halo over my shoulder and walked to the car, an old school 1980 Chevy Malibu. I tossed Halo's limp body in the back using zip ties to secure Halo's legs and arms.

I'll be damned if I got attacked from the back seat while trying to get where I was going.

Once I knew I was good, I slid behind the wheel and turned the car on. I pulled out the driveway like shit was good. So far, there was no police anywhere and no nosy ass neighbors. I drove off completely oblivious to somebody watching me. I drove to the stop sign and made a left turn. I turned on to Austin Avenue making a left and heading towards the e-way. I drove the speed limit and everything. Last thing I needed was to be pulled over when I had somebody tied up in the back seat.

I glided on to the I-290 and headed South. I was going out to a house I had in Alsip. It was smooth sailing at this time of night. I made it to 127th Street in no time and got off on my exit. I made a right turn on to Ridgeway Avenue. I kept straight until I got where I was going. I made another right turn on to 128th Street and pulled into a small Tudor style home. I pulled into the garage and cut the ignition off. I waited until the garage door closed all the way before I got Halo out.

I snatched Halo's limp body from the back seat

and tossed 'em over my shoulder. I walked inside the house through the garage door and went straight to the basement. I tossed Halo down on the table I had set up and cuffed Halo's arms and legs after cutting the zip ties off. Halo was lying face down on the table. I rolled Halo over because that was just what I wanted. I sat back in the chair next to the table and waited. I knew it wouldn't be long before Halo came to. The first thing I wanted that muthafucka to see was my face.

***

24 hours later....

This muthafucka still wasn't awake. Halo moaned a little here and there but still hadn't woken up. I was past irritated, but time didn't wait for no man. I went upstairs and found the mop bucket in the pantry that Dee used to use. I filled it with cold water and walked back downstairs with it. I got to the bottom of the stairs and stomped over to the table I had Halo strapped down to. I tossed the cold water on Halo and waited for it to work. Halo came to with a startled expression.

"The fuck? Let me off this shit, my nigga! I swear

you're fuckin' dead!"

"You talk a lot of shit for somebody who's in no shape to talk."

"Fuck you, homeboy! What kinda nigga does shit like this? Take me one on one like a real nigga would. You ain't shit but a bitch."

"Ha, the real bitch here is you," I said laughing. "C'mon Halo, baby, how long did you think you could do this shit and nobody cut you off? This game ain't no place for you. You just need to mind your own business."

"This is my fuckin' business. This is my blood, my nigga! My daddy bred me for this shit. It ain't my fault you ain't nothin' but a bum ass nigga. Yo' daddy wasn't shit but a snake. Like father, like son, huh? If you was a real nigga, you'd take me head up!" Halo spat.

I just laughed before walking over and punching Halo in the mouth. Fuck nigga was really trying me right now, but I had the upper hand. I was gonna enjoy torturing this muthafucka before finally ending shit. I grabbed the syringe I had sitting on the table and injected Halo with it. Muthafucka had me fucked up, but guess what? Halo was gon' learn today! These were my streets, and I wasn't giving them up to nobody. Fuck Halo. Fuck Bread. Fuck Butta, and fuck The Faction. This shit was about to be my city. All them niggas could get it.

Chapter Twenty

True

I went over to Halo's house so I could keep an eye out on shit. I knew bro was mad at me, but I still felt like the shit was stupid. I couldn't control what these hoes did out here nor did I remember every bitch I smashed. Halo knew me better than anybody, and one thing about me was that I never kept the same bitch around twice unless shit was that good. That's why Honesty had been around as long as she had been. Other than her, all the other bitches were just a smash and dash.

I parked my car a few houses up from Halo's spot. I sat there for a good minute before nodding off. I woke up when I heard gunshots and shit. Since it was dark, I couldn't clearly see who was coming out the house unless I was actually in the yard. Somebody came out with something slung over their shoulder. Everything in me said to follow this car, so I did. I stayed back at a safe distance and fell four cars behind the Chevy Malibu. It merged on to I-290, so I followed suit. I drove behind that muthafucka all the way to Alsip. The fuck?

I watched as the car pulled into a small home. I had to drive past the house so as not to arouse suspicion. Fuck! I wanted so badly to rush the house, but I didn't know who all might be in there or what might be waiting for me. I drove back towards Halo's house to see what the fuck was really good. If this muthafucka had done something to Halo, then it was death for sure for that nigga. I headed back towards the e-way and took that ride.

It was late, so the roads were clear. When I pulled up at Halo's house, I saw the front door standing wide open. I pulled my gun and walked inside cautiously. I looked around and saw shit in disarray. I followed the damage up the stairs. That's when I saw Halo's bedroom door splintered to pieces. I walked in the room hoping to find some type of clue or evidence to point me in the direction of who did this but found nothing. I went back downstairs pissed off because my best friend was gone, and I didn't know what the fuck to think.

When I walked outside, I saw nosy ass, Ms. Mary, sitting on her porch. Once she saw me, she damn near flew down her walkway. She waved me down and stopped in front of me breathing hard as fuck. I thought her ass was having a heart attack. I slowed down so I wouldn't knock her over and waited for her to talk.

"Oooohhhh shit, chile, hol' up. Lemme catch my breath. Whooo."

"What's good, Ms. Mary? I don't have a lot of time."

"I already know that, fool. Hush up. Lemme talk.

I stood still and listened to what she had to say.

"Some crazy nigga came over here and broke into your friend's house. Lilo was shouting out the window, and I heard a gunshot or some shit."

"You mean Halo?"

"You know what the hell I meant, chile. Anywho, like I said, I heard a shot and some yelling, but I was too scared to come outside to see what the hell was going on. Some brown skinned nigga, I think y'all know him, had that child slung over his shoulder. Drove outta here like his ass was on fire or something."

"What did dude look like?"

"He's the same one that been around that chile for years. Lilo, Halo, what the hell ever that chile's name is; that other boy been around for a long time. They daddies used to hang with each other back in the day."

"Thanks, Ms. Mary."

That was all the confirmation I needed. Deuce's bitch ass had Halo, and I knew where they were. I called Bread and Butta. Shit was on and popping, because tonight, Deuce was a dead man.

***

We agreed to meet at the hospital since that's where they were anyway. There was still no word on Beauty, but the kids were doing better. Bryce's surgery went well, and Brandon Jr. was even starting to feel his legs. Brennen didn't really know what was going on, but he kept crying for his mama and his twin, Brianna. Shit was all fucked up, and now Deuce had Halo. What the fuck man?

When I walked into Beauty's hospital room, I could tell something was wrong. Bread had his head down, and he was crying. Butta was holding Baby, and she was holding Brennen. Lil' man was hollering loud as shit. I took my nephew from her arms, and she almost fell over. I tried to calm Brennen down, but I had to ask the obvious question.

"Yo, what the hell is going on?"

"She gone, man," Bread answered still sobbing.

"Who gone? I know you ain't sayin' what I think you sayin'."

"She flat-lined after you called. They just stopped doing CPR on her. How the fuck I'ma tell m-my k-k-kids 'bout they m-mama?"

The last time I heard a scream like that was when Halo lost Storm and Bread lost his lil' girl. I couldn't even imagine was the big homie was going through right now. He just lost his daughter and wife back to back. I hated to be the bearer of even more bad news, but I had to tell what was going on.

"I know now is a bad time, but Halo is missing."

Both of the twins snapped their heads in my

direction. "Fuck you mean?" they said in unison.

"Me and Halo got into some shit after we took care of Dee. That's a whole 'nother story I'll tell you later, but long story short, shorty was the one gassin' Deuce up to cause drama. We took care of her rat ass, but now this nigga Deuce done went and snatched up Halo. I followed his ass to a house out in Alsip, but without back-up, I didn't wanna run up in the house. I need y'all niggas with me."

"Bet that. Let's do this shit. I owe that nigga a few bullets to the head for my wife and daughter," Bread responded.

I handed Brennen over to Baby. She looked at Butta with pleading eyes, but she knew what shit was. I gave Bread some time to square shit away with his wife. While he took care of his business, I left to get the shit ready that we would need. This was definitely war, and Deuce was gonna be dead after this. I just hoped that we got there in time before something happened to Halo.

Bread hit my line to let me know him, and Butta was ready, so I hit 'em with the address. I had everything we needed in the van I was driving. I hit the e-way, and we met up a few blocks away from the house where Deuce had Halo at. We all got suited up and made the rest of the trek on foot. Last thing we needed was some nosy ass person seeing us in front of that house. I was gonna take the front, and the twins were gonna take the back.

We stopped just short of the driveway. There were some shrubs right next to it that gave us some protection, but it was dark as fuck outside too. We split up seeing if we could find a way inside without alerting Deuce that we were there. I walked up to the front door paranoid as fuck. I kept looking around thinking somebody was gonna hop out the bushes or some shit. I tried the doorknob first, and surprisingly, it was unlocked. I twisted it and went inside.

I crept towards the back door staying vigilante. I turned the knob, and that door was unlocked too. It was like this fuck nigga was taunting us or some shit by leaving the doors unlocked. We searched the first floor and found nothing. I stayed at the bottom of the stairs while Bread and Butta searched the second floor.

They came back down and said there was nothing there. We all split up and looked around to see if there was a basement door or something. Halo had to be in this damn house.

I walked into the kitchen and checked everything. I whistled real quick when I found another door inside the pantry. That was some slick ass shit. I woulda never thought to find a basement door inside the pantry. The twins found where I was and followed my lead. I slowly pulled the door opened and took the first step. I listened as hard as I could for any indication that someone was in the basement. I heard some smacking and a whole lot of grunting and yelling. The fuck was going on?

Chapter Twenty-One

Deuce

Halo was still knocked out, so that gave me time to set shit up. I cut off all Halo's clothes, and the muthafucka was asshole naked on the table. I took my time on some creep shit. I took my hand and rubbed it up Halo's leg all the way to the top of Halo's face. Halo was awake now and unsure of what the fuck was going to happen. I had to put a gag in that muthafucka's mouth because of all the screaming. The fear in Halo's eyes had my dick brick hard.

I stared heavily at Halo's body. Wasn't no better way to fuck somebody's head up then take their shit from them. With Halo tied up, I undid my belt buckle and dropped my pants. I stroked my hard dick and climbed on top of the table. Halo squirmed underneath me, but I didn't give not one fuck. I was about to enjoy this shit. I don't give a fuck what y'all think. I rammed my dick in Halo and started talkin' shit.

"Yeah, bitch. Talk all that tough ass shit now. I

told you I was gon' make you my bitch. Damn, this shit here. Halo, you been holdin' out on a nigga all this time? Fuck, I'm 'bout to cum."

Just as I bust my nut, I was hit over the back of the head hard as fuck. I fell off the table and Halo. I looked up to see three guns in my face. I shoulda known True's ass was gon' sniff behind this bitch until Halo was found. I was hit again, but I still laughed evilly.

"Fuck all y'all niggas. Whole time you been takin' orders from a bitch! Yo, that pussy hittin' too!" I said before I was hit again.

Bread and Butta had their guns trained on me as I laughed. True cut the zip ties on Halo's hands and feet then passed her a gun. Yes, Halo was a *her*. The whole time I was the only one who knew this shit 'cuz we grew up together. Before her mama passed away, she dressed like a girl. After that, she went straight tomboy. She never really filled out, so niggas never really knew she was a girl.

Her pops raised her like a lil' boy. She dressed like a nigga, walked like a nigga, and talked like a nigga. I always knew that Halo was gon' do bigger shit than me, but I always thought I could tame her ass. After all, she was a bitch, and all bitches could be controlled. All I needed was the opportunity to put that lil' bitch in her place, but now, I see the mistake I made.

Halo climbed off the table, naked as the day she was born, and walked over to where the twins had me hemmed up against the wall. True passed her a gun, and I didn't even flinch when she put the shit to my head. I spit in her face knowing that would ultimately disrespect her. She wiped it off with her hand and wiped her hand on my shirt. She cocked the .45 in her hand and blasted off two shots.

My body slid down the wall I was up against, and my eyes closed. I was no more. In my last fleeting thoughts, all I could think was that a bitch got the best of me.

Chapter Twenty-Two

Halo

The cat was out the fuckin' bag! My niggas knew I was a female, but they didn't flinch not one time when I bodied Deuce. Bread and Butta were standing behind me, but True wasn't. I didn't know where that nigga went, but at the time, I gave no fucks. I was who I was, and I wasn't ashamed about the shit. That's part of the reason I went so hard. My daddy always told me that the game would be twice as hard for me because I was a female, so I needed to act like a nigga.

I acted like a nigga so much so that even my closest niggas didn't know I was a female. True had been my nigga for a good minute, but even he didn't know my true identity. Bread and Butta looked like it didn't even phase them. I looked back at Deuce's brains splattered across the wall and just shrugged. I started looking around the basement for some clothes or something I could cover up with. I heard footsteps on the stairs and raised my gun. When I saw that it was True, I lowered my shit.

"Here bruh, I thought you might need this shit," he said tossing me a shirt and some sweats.

"Good looking out," I said as I dressed.

The guys gave me some privacy by turning their backs the whole time. I wasn't embarrassed though. I was who I was. Wasn't no shame in my shit. I got dressed and let them know it was good to turn around. True walked over to me and dapped me up. Bread and Butta did the same thing. We filed out the basement without saying a word. As Bread and Butta led me down the street and away from the house, True doubled back. When we got to the van, I saw what True did. The street was ablaze. The entire house was engulfed in flames as we picked True up and drove off.

We drove back towards the e-way and headed back towards the hospital. I could lie and say that I was all good, but I knew that I wasn't. My mental was already fucked up over losing Storm, and then Deuce pulled this shit. I had never been violated like that before. Maybe that's because, for the longest time, niggas thought I was a nigga. I had portrayed one long enough too that nobody really thought about it. I knew my niggas wanted to speak on it, but I guess the look on my face let they asses know that now wasn't the time.

We got to the hospital about forty-five minutes later. I walked into the emergency room all fucked up and started crying. I walked over to the desk and got the attention of a nurse. I was crying hard as fuck because shit just hit me. She looked up at me and asked if she could help me.

"Yes. I was beat up and raped," I said out loud breaking down.

I fell to the floor, and the nurse rushed from around the desk to help me. Shit sounded so different saying the shit out loud. I thought I could handle it, but clearly, I couldn't. I lay on the floor crying my eyes out--crying for my mama, crying for my daddy, crying for Storm, crying for me. All I had was me now. Everybody I had ever loved was gone. Who was gon' take care of me?

Another nurse came to help the first one to get me off the ground. I was led to the back right away and put in a bed. The first nurse did all she could to try to soothe me as the second nurse set everything up to start a rape kit and get me tested for any STD's. I really didn't want to comply, but I knew I had to in order to make sure that I was straight.

I lay on the bed in a room still in my clothes. The nurse explained to me that she needed me to change into a gown so they could do an examination. She left a gown and a blanket at the foot of the bed and left with the other nurse. I waited until they left and undressed crying the whole time. This was some shit I never thought I'd ever have to go through. I was Halo, head of The Faction and feared all over the Chi. Now, here I was in a hospital getting ready to get poked and prodded because I was raped.

I lay in the cold hospital room on that hard ass bed and thought about everything that happened recently. Storm was killed. Beauty had been in an accident. Brianna didn't make it, and two of the other kids had serious injuries. Dee was dead. Deuce was dead, and I was done. If he wanted it, True could have this shit, because I was over it. There was a knock on the door, and a female doctor walked in along with the nurse who helped me into the room. She introduced herself and explained everything that she had to do to check me out.

I stayed quiet the whole time while tears streamed down my face. The nurse stood next to me holding my hand and rubbing my head. The doctor must've sensed that I needed that support, so she didn't have the nurse to assist her in the examination. When it was done, I rolled over and cried my eyes out. I must've fallen asleep because when I woke up, True was sitting in the chair next to my bed quietly. I looked away from him hating to look weak to him.

"You gon' be good, fam. This don't change shit between us. You still my nigga," True said.

"But still, I hid that shit from y'all 'cuz I didn't want y'all to look at me funny," I said wiping my tears.

"Did you put in the work? Were you busting guns with us? Whole bloodlines, remember, my nigga? WE did that! YOU DID THAT! Ain't no difference in us, bruh. You good."

No words were spoken after that. We sat in silence until I drifted back off to sleep. Strangely enough, True never left my side the whole time. When the doctor came back into the room several hours later to tell me the results, he asked me if I wanted him to step out. I told him no and asked the doctor to just give it to me straight. She let me know that I was clear of all STD's including HIV and AIDS. I let go of the breath I was holding. She told me that it was imperative to get tested every six months for at least the next two years to be sure that I was clear from HIV and AIDS.

I still didn't know how to process everything. I was glad that I didn't have anything, but look at me. I was big, badass Halo. I put fear in people, not the other way around, and here I was reduced to a crying mess in a hospital bed after getting raped by someone I thought was family. When the fuck did Deuce get like this? I tried to think back to anyone incident where I noticed a change, but I couldn't remember one.

As if shit wasn't fucked up already, True dropped a bomb on me. Beauty had died while I was missing. I already knew how Bread was feeling because I was still grieving over Storm's death. It came as no surprise to me when he sent word through True that he was out the game. He told True that before all this shit happened Beauty was talking about moving to North Carolina. He was going out there next week to look at properties after he talked to his cousin Laz.

I couldn't blame bro for his decision. After losing so much, I would leave too. I would miss his ass though. Halo loved the kids, so I had to make sure to keep in contact with him when it came to the boys. Butta and Baby were going too. I knew that was going to happen because they were twins. They did everything together. With Baby being pregnant with twins of her own, I didn't blame Butta for wanting her protected too. Everybody deserved to be happy. They had been in the game a good sixteen years. They deserved to retire in peace.

Now all I had to do was figure out how to tell True that everything was his. North Carolina didn't seem like a bad place to go, but I didn't wanna leave my nigga naked like that in the Chi. I was gonna stay behind and get True straight. I wasn't gonna be in the streets no more, but if he ever needed me, I'd come out of retirement for True. Once a legend, always a legend.

***

I was discharged a few hours later with a few meds for pain and prevention of any diseases. I told True to take me to a hotel. I wanted to be somewhere lowkey as fuck where nobody knew me. He drove me out to Elmhurst on Grand Avenue and County Line Road to the Country Inn & Suites. I paid the bullshit eighty-five-dollars a night for the room for two weeks. I made it up to my room and fell back on the bed. We had hit a Walmart before we got here, so I had the basic shit that I needed. I knew I could get ghost for a minute and be good. True was in charge for now.

I tossed all my bags to the side and sat up. I looked around thinking about the little ass room I was in. Never had I ever been reduced to some shit like this. I was always living lavish, and despite the fact that I had more than one home to go to, I didn't want to be in either of them right now. They both reminded me too much of Storm, and I didn't need that shit. I just wanted to relax and de-stress. I already knew I was gonna cry a lot. I really didn't know how to feel anymore.

I took off my clothes and walked into the bathroom. I turned the water on so I could take a shower. I caught my reflection in the mirror, and for the first time in my life, I became self-conscious of my body. I saw the bruises and shit from when Deuce beat on me. I twisted and turned looking at every angle of my body. Shit was sad because I never felt like a female, but I loved the hell outta the female form. I stayed in front of the mirror until the steam from the shower fogged the mirror up.

Getting in the shower, I cried some more. I cried for what happened, what was, and what would never be again. I cried for Storm knowing that she didn't deserve to die or the way it happened. I knew it would take a whole lot of time for me to get over her death if I ever did. Storm always knew who I was and what I was. We always had plans for a family and everything else despite it all. Now I could understand why True was the way he was. My heart was gonna stay guarded because I couldn't go through this type of shit again.

I washed up scrubbing my skin until it turned red. I could still smell Deuce on me. I felt like it was reeking from my pores. My skin was raw by the time I got out the shower, and I still smelled him. I rolled a blunt and poured me a drink hoping to get so fucked up that I could get some sleep. I was faded, so I laid down and closed my eyes. I jumped up the minute that I did. I saw Deuce's face with that fucked up look looking down at me while he raped me.

That shit sounded so fuckin' foreign for me to be saying. I was raped. A nigga like me was raped. I was spazzing the fuck out, and I couldn't do shit about it. I would have to try my best to get over this shit. It might take a while, but I wasn't about to let what this nigga did to me beat me in any type of way. I finally fell asleep from exhaustion.

"You gon' be good, bae, I promise. You'll get over this."

"Storm bae, why did you leave me?"

"It was just my time to go. I didn't want to, but I had to."

"But I need you, bae. I can't do this without you."

"You'll be fine, bae. I know you will."

"Just come back. Please come back to me, bae."

"I love you, Halo. Never ever forget that."

I woke up screaming Storm's name knowing that I was dreaming. I just wanted my old life back. I wanted my woman back. Hell, I wanted my daddy back. I knew that if he were here, none of this shit would've ever happened. I cried again and so hard that I fell back to sleep.

Chapter Twenty-Three

Bread

Before we pulled the shit off with Deuce, I spent my last few hours with my wife that I would ever have with her again. I was gonna have her cremated as well so she could always be with me. I hit my cousin Laz up in North Carolina to let him know I was moving down there. After all the shit that happened up here, I owed it to Beauty to take my sons somewhere safe that I could raise them. I just wanted to make my wife proud of me.

After Beauty's cremation, I started separating myself from The Faction. Halo went ghost, but we all understood why. I did the same thing she did and handed my shit over to True. Shit was crazy finding out that Halo was a female, but it didn't change how I looked at her. She was thorough as fuck. She was more thorough than the niggas who claimed they were. She put in that work, so she earned every ounce of respect that she got from me.

I had just strapped Brennen in his car seat so we

could leave. I took one last look at the house that my wife and I shared. I was gonna miss that woman with everything in me. Maybe one day I would find somebody to occupy my time but never my heart. Beauty was my one and only. There was no way I'd love another woman the way that I loved her. Would I fuck somebody else? For sure, because I was a man who had needs. I got in the van I rented, cranked it up, and pulled off.

The U-Haul was already on the road to North Carolina. We were moving to Greensboro. Laz and his wife, Kai, had houses all over North Carolina. Since they never really stayed in their house in Greensboro, we were staying there until I found us a spot. I appreciated Laz for looking out for us. He was the last cousin we had on our father's side of the family. Him and his father, Larenz, were all my brother and I had left.

I wanted to give my sons a new outlook on life. Shit was about to be different. I didn't want them to know shit about this street life. I wanted their asses to be real squares. Lawyers, doctors, and all that good shit. I didn't want them to be like me. I wanted them to be better than me. Plus, I didn't want my wife haunting my ass for letting them get into the streets. I laughed to myself at that thought.

I merged on to I-90/94 heading East. Once we passed the Skyway, I knew we were outta Chicago. All the memories I had flooded through my memory. I hit my first lick here. Hit my first bitch here. Sold my first brick here. Caught my first body here. Found my wife here. Had my kids here. Almost lost my whole family here. Lost my wife and daughter here. There was a lot of good shit, but it was a lot of bad shit too. This move was gonna be good for us. I could feel it.

We stopped in Kentucky to get some rest and wash up. I got us a room and fed my sons. After bathing them and putting them to sleep, I took care of myself. I ate and hopped in the shower. It was then that I finally cried. I cried long and hard so I could get it all out my system. My wife and daughter were gone. How the fuck was a nigga supposed to get over that? I knew I wouldn't, and if I did, it would be years before it happened.

I finished up in the shower and got out. I threw some clothes on and got in the bed. I laid there wide awake for a long ass time while I listened to my son's sleep. This wasn't how life was supposed to go for me. I should've listened to Beauty a long ass time ago when she wanted us to leave. That was my fault though. If my sons ever came and told me some shit that they thought was detrimental to their way of life, I would listen. I don't know when I fell asleep, but I finally did.

I woke up to my son on the bed with me. Brennen was jumping up and down next to me holding on to the headboard. Brandon Jr. and Bryce were laying in the bed still quietly watching cartoons. I had to make sure that my sons got the best treatment they needed when we got to North Carolina. I had even hired a nurse to accompany us on this trip just to be safe. She was being paid handsomely for assisting me. I would send her on a flight back to Chicago once the boys were situated, and I had a new nurse.

I got up, got the boys ready, and got myself ready. I knocked on the room next door to let the nurse I needed her to sit with the boys while I took everything to the van. She was already ready, so she obliged me. It took two trips to get everything in the van. I came back to the room and picked up Brandon Jr. and Bryce. She carried Brennen, and we left. Once they were inside the van and good, we pulled off to finish our trip. We should be in North Carolina by nightfall. We only had eight more hours to go.

We arrived at a little after nine o'clock that night. We all were exhausted, and the boys were cranky. The nurse helped me with the boys and returned to her room for the night. I laid the boys in bed with me. I didn't want to be far away from them. I didn't want them to wake up scared either especially in a new home. We fell asleep, and visions of my wife danced in my dreams.

Chapter Twenty-Four

Butta

After all the shit my family went through, I decided to follow my brother to North Carolina. My wife was pregnant, and I didn't need her to stress herself out and lose my babies. I wanted shit to be so smooth that she didn't notice anything bad. Besides, without my twin near me, I knew I would feel lost. Having a bond with your brother was one thing, but having a twin was something else. He was my best friend.

When I told Baby we were going to North Carolina with Bread and my nephews, she was cool with it. We tied up all our loose ends and flew down there. My cousin Laz picked us up in Raleigh at the airport and drove us out to the house in Greensboro that he said we could stay at with Bread and the boys. The house was big as fuck with seven bedrooms, six bathrooms, a den, dining room, two living rooms, a library, an office and a bunch of other shit. I found a room for me and Baby and settled in. I knew Bread wouldn't be there till the next day.

When I woke up that next morning, it was like everything hit me all at once. My sister-in-law was gone. My niece was gone. I was out the game. I was about to be a father. I was happy, and I didn't have to watch my back anymore. Finally, life was how it should be. Baby was already up exploring the house, so I rolled a blunt after taking a piss and got lifted. My stomach started growling so I went to go find the kitchen and get some food. My wife must've known I was gonna be hungry because she was already cooking. Shit smelled good as hell too.

I crept over to her and slid my hands around her growing belly. Since she was carrying twins, her belly was poking out already at only four months. I couldn't wait to see what we were having. I was excited as hell to be a daddy. I saw the joy it gave my brother when it came to his kids, and I wanted that shit too. I kissed Baby on her neck and smacked her on the ass before sitting down at the table. She hooked a nigga up with some steak and eggs.

She brought me my plate and sat hers down

across from me. She turned around to get our drinks and paused. Her hands went to her belly, and I immediately thought something was wrong. I jumped up so damn quick almost knocking the table over trying to rush to her.

"Baby, are you ok? Is it the twins? Are y'all good?"

She turned to me with tears in her eyes and grabbed my hand placing it on her belly. I felt little flutters and smiled. My babies were kicking for the first time. I was so happy to be able to share this experience with my wife. It was the best feeling in the fuckin' world. I led her back to the table, and I got our drinks. We said grace and talked about baby names while we ate.

"If it's two girls, I want their names to be Beauty and Lil', Baby."

"Two of y'all again? Hell nah!" I laughed.

"Why not? I wanna name my babies after me and sis. What's so bad about that?"

"Mannnnn, y'all spoiled as hell. Having daughters would be even worse."

"You already know they gon' be spoiled, so I don't even know why you trippin'."

"Yeah, yeah. If it's two boys, I want my Junior and my other son can be named Brayden."

"What if it's a girl and a boy?"

"Then it's Junior and Beauty. Lord, I ask you now to please give me two sons because if you give me a daughter, she's gonna be single till I die." I fake prayed.

Baby laughed at me while we finished our food. For the first time in a long time, I was good. My wife was happy, my babies were good, and I was secure in the decision that I made. This was how life should be. I had seen my wife cry more times than I ever wanted her to cry in life. From now on, if she was crying, it would be happy tears only.

Chapter Twenty-Five

True

If somebody woulda told me a year ago that all this shit was gonna happen, I wouldn't have believed shit they said. I didn't see none of it coming besides getting rid of Deuce since he was fucking up so much. Now here I was running Chicago with the blessing from Halo, Bread, and Butta. They had me set up real nice. The Faction was no more, but the respect for it was still present. Everybody didn't need to know the specifics of shit; all they knew was that I was in charge.

I had been ripping and running so much that I didn't know whether I was coming or going. Trying to get shit right after Deuce's fuck up caused me to handle quite a few niggas. Once I was sure that everything was back good, I decided to focus on what I had going on with Honesty. Shorty had proved that she was solid, but I was still skeptical. After all, I hadn't been in a relationship in a long ass time.

After Kalila was killed, I didn't wanna open

myself up to anybody because of how I felt after I buried her. I felt like I buried my heart with my woman the day she was put in the ground. Honesty was trying her best to prove to me that she was right for me, but I still couldn't let the wall around my heart down. I wanted to, but something kept stopping me.

Trying to be king of some shit and working on a relationship was hard fuckin' work! Halo had went completely ghost on everybody. I knew she checked into that little bullshit hotel I took her to, but after calling her repeatedly to check on her and not getting an answer, I went there. I found out that she checked out early despite paying to stay there for two weeks. Her ass was gone with the wind, and I had no way of finding her. I knew when she wanted to be found, she'd hit me up. I was gonna miss her though. That was my nigga.

I was on my way to pick up Honesty from work. I couldn't believe it when shorty told me she was a paralegal. Like she was real life the shit. Shorty was on her grind hard and was even taking classes at Loyola University School of Law in order to obtain her law degree. I was getting to know more about her feisty ass, and it was cool. I still didn't wanna let my guard down with her because I felt like I would be betraying Kalila. She was still cool to kick it with though. I would just have to see how shit goes.

I pulled up in front of Neal & Leroy Law Offices, LLC. and parked. Shorty had about ten more minutes before the end of her shift, so I waited. While I was sitting there waiting, some dude rolled up on me and knocked on my window.

"Hey man, I'ont want no smoke. I just saw you and took a chance on speaking to you."

"What's good?" I asked gripping my pistol.

"Like I said, I'ont want no smoke. I just wanna chance to get down."

"Why should I give you one?" I asked him.

" 'Cuz a nigga out here hungry. I'm all my family got. I got a lil' sister who needs me, and my mama ain't shit."

"Where ya' pops at?"

"That nigga been gone as soon as my mama told him she was pregnant with my sister. He ain't never come back, and after my sister was born, my mama went downhill. She addicted and don't give no fucks about us. I can't let my sister grow up like that."

"How old are you and your sister?"

"I'm seventeen, and she's nine. Please True, lemme prove myself to you, fam. I'll do anything."

"You know what? I'ma give you a chance, but if you fuck me over, I'ma kill you straight like that. Meet me at this address tomorrow and bring your sister with you. Leave all the shit like clothes and whatever and bring only the shit that means something to you. You work for me now, and a man that don't put in work don't get to eat like that. I'ma put y'all up, but you owe me now."

"Thanks so much, man. I really appreciate this shit, and I swear I won't let you down."

"One more thing."

"Yeah, what's up?"

"What's ya' name, kid?"

"They call me Savage."

"Bet that. Tomorrow. One o'clock, and don't be late. I'll see you then."

Just as I finished with Savage, Honesty came waltzing out the building. Shorty was bad as fuck, and my dick bricked up just looking at her sexy ass. She walked up looking at Savage with a major side eye and got in the car. She slid down in the seat and nodded at the kid.

"What's that about?"

"Just a shorty needing some help. I'ma need you to help me with him and his sister."

"Help how?"

"I'm sending them to your spot tomorrow. I need you to let them stay with you till I can see how shorty moves. If he puts in the work, then I'll get them their own spot."

"I swear, you such a good dude, but your reputation makes you seem like a monster."

"Nah, I just can recognize another real ass person. He's just trying to take care of himself and his sister."

"I got you, baby," Honesty said leaning over to kiss me.

I pulled off, and we headed to the mall. I

grabbed basic stuff for shorty and his sister like body wash, socks, towels, washcloths, and some other shit that Honesty said his sister might want. We scooped some food and headed to Honesty's crib.

***

The next day, at ten minutes to one, Savage showed up with a little girl. Honesty let them in while I sat in her small office. On her desk, I had a few stacks of money, two guns, and some work. It was a test, but I wanted to see what Savage would pick first. Whatever he picked first would let me know what type of dude he was. By default, I'd give him the other two if he chose the right one. Honesty showed him into the office and left us alone.

"What's good, Savage? Have a seat."

I walked around the desk and leaned in front of it. "You said you hungry, right? How hungry are you?"

"I'm fuckin' starving, bro. Just let me know what you need me to do, and I got you."

"You see these three things?" I said motioning to the desk. "You have a choice to pick one. Pick the right one, and you in with me. Pick the wrong one, and I'll body your ass. Choose wisely."

I stepped away from the desk and watched as he got out of his seat. He didn't even hesitate and chose the work. He looked at me after he did.

"Give me an hour, and I'll be back. What's the return you want on this?"

"Good job, shorty. Here you go," I said handing him both guns and the money. He looked at me shocked.

"What's this about? I'ont want no sympathy or nothing, bro. Just let me get this work off. Lemme prove to you what I can do."

"You just did. Consider this a signing bonus. Now, you ready to work?"

"Hell yeah!"

I sat back and chopped it up with Savage for the rest of the afternoon. Honesty was chilling with his sister who I later found out was named Kaliyah. Shit had me shook because she kinda looked like Kalila. I shook the thought off and let it go. Both of them were cool as fuck. I could see something great in Savage, and if I had anything to do with it, I'd make sure to get him right.

Chapter Twenty-Six

Honesty

I really didn't know what to think when it came to True. We had been dealing with each other for some time, but it was mostly a fuck type of thing with us. I knew I started to have feelings for him when he called about that nigga Deuce. He offered me ten bands to get the drop on the nigga, and I did. Afterwards, when we linked up, I didn't even ask about the money. He did my body so right that night even though he knew what I just did with Deuce.

I don't know where this will go or if it will go anywhere period, but I'm willing to try since he is. I know I got big shoes to fill since his last girl was killed, but I wanna try. As he could see, I get my own bag. His money is just a bonus because I'd rather have his heart. When I saw him talking to that young kid outside my job, I was in awe. I told him I would help him with whatever he needed, and I did.

When Savage and Kaliyah showed up at my

place the next afternoon, I kicked it with her while
Savage politicked with True. They came out a few
hours later smiling and laughing, so that means shit
was all good. When I introduced True to Kaliyah, he
looked like he saw a ghost, but he didn't say anything.
I'll keep that to myself though. My baby been stressed
enough, and he doesn't need any more shit.

Halo is gone in the wind, and the twins moved
down south. True really is out here in these streets by
himself. I think he chose Savage because he needs
somebody dependable and trustworthy. He saw
something in him that makes him believe he is. I felt
bad for him because I know he missed Halo. That was
his best friend. It didn't matter that Halo was a girl.
Yes, he told me. I started to go looking for her, but True
told me to leave it alone. He said when Halo was ready,
she'd come back.

So, here I was, in love. I had it bad for my hitta,
but he doesn't know I love him yet. Tonight he will
though. Tonight is the night that I bare my soul.
Hopefully, it won't all be for nothing. You ain't gotta
wait a lifetime to find a man who you know is worthy.

You just gotta wait for the right time.

Chapter Twenty-Seven

Baby

These last few months have been a rollercoaster of shit. Just like my husband, I had lost a sister and a niece but gained twins of my own. I was four months pregnant and getting bigger each day. We moved when Bread did. I would follow my husband to the ends of the earth and back, so I didn't even protest the move at all. I was loving the new city I was in, and their cousin's wife was the shit. I could see why Laz loved her the way that he did.

There was a month left before the end of the year, and I was ready to ring in 2017 with a bang. Even though I couldn't drink, my New Year's was still gonna be lit! I had everything I needed right here where I was at. It couldn't get any better than this unless God was granting wishes and he's give us back Beauty and Brianna. I still cried over losing them, so I could only imagine how it affected Bread and the boys. They still kept asking for their mama and Brianna.

I felt my babies kick for the first time, and I was over the moon happy. I couldn't wait to see what we were having. At this point, I didn't even care what sex they were as long as they were healthy. I noticed that we didn't talk much about my pregnancy around Bread, but I understood why Butta didn't want us to. He was trying to be sympathetic towards his brother until Bread checked his ass and told him he better get happy about his kids. I laughed so hard at him for that.

Kai was throwing me a baby shower. Her sons' girlfriends were helping out. Since Saphirre was on her boss shit, I let her handle the glam part since baby girl had a great eye for decorations. Queen was very mature for her age, and she loved to cook and eat just like her boo thang. She was gonna take care of the menu. Kai was getting the venue, DJ, and invitations. All I had to do was show my happy ass up.

It was fun getting to know Butta's people these last couple of days. Even though we just got here, I felt like I was at home. Not even back in Chicago did I feel like that. Maybe it was the energy down here, or maybe it was the serene ass setting. We had mountains damn near in the backyard. The view was breathtaking. The back porch was already becoming my favorite place to be because of the view.

If we could live here for the rest of our lives and never move again, I'd be happy as hell, but who knows what the future holds. I just wanted to get fat, be happy, love on my husband, and let him love me and our babies back.

Chapter Twenty-Seven

Halo

February 2016

These last few months have been wild as fuck. If anybody woulda told me back in March that by the end of the year this woulda happened, I wouldn't believe that shit. Even losing my girl wasn't a thought until the shit actually happened.

Getting caught up by Deuce and getting raped definitely wasn't thought of. I had to go ghost on everybody because I had to find myself. I felt some type of way and didn't know how to keep my emotions in check.

The only one who'd ever seen that side of me was Storm. Now I was an emotional ass wreck all day every day. I was ducked off in Southern Illinois where nobody knew me, and I didn't know anybody. I liked it that way because I didn't have to watch my back, and it was safer that way.

I had to concentrate on getting my mental right after everything, and it didn't make it no better that I was now pregnant. I was only six months along, but I was having a little girl. I was gonna name her Storm and do my best to do right by her. I had more than enough money to live nice off thanks to my daddy and myself.

Once I had the baby, I had plans to reach out to all my people. I knew they were all probably worried to death about me. I had changed my number and everything. Mental health is everything, lemme tell you. If ya' mental ain't right, then you can't be right.

I just hoped that the next four months went by quick as shit. I didn't know nothin' about a baby or being a mom, but I was gonna do what I had to do.

***

Four months later

I woke up that morning with pain every fuckin' where. I called 911 because there was no way I could make it anywhere by myself. I was lucky I made it to open the front door for the paramedics. I laid on the floor near my front door with it wide open. The day was June 14, 2016. Today was Storm's birthday.

The paramedics arrived in no time and got me in the back of the ambulance while they shot off questions. I answered them as best as I could. The pain was unbearable, and there was no way in hell this would ever happen again. I loved my lil' girl, but she damn sure wasn't getting no brother or sister unless I got with another chick that had kids.

My daughter wasn't waiting for anybody, and on the way to the hospital, she was born in the back of the ambulance at three-twenty that afternoon. I did it all with no pain meds or nothing. By the time we got to the hospital, I was begging the doctor to take out my uterus.

We were all comfortable in our room when I pulled my cell phone out the bag that one of the medics grabbed for me being locking my house up. I dialed a number I had committed to memory and waited patiently for an answer.

"Yo, what's good?

"My muthafuckin' nigga. What's good with you?" I said happily into the phone.

"Halo? That's you? Yo, I swear to God it was like you disappeared off the face of the earth. I looked everywhere for you, man. You still my nigga. Where you at?"

"I'm in the hospital."

"You good? We got beef?"

"Nah True, chill. I was just calling because I thought you'd like to come meet your niece."

"My niece? What you went and got you a ch-"

It was like it suddenly clicked in his head what I was telling him. I was kinda scared of his reaction because he was my best friend.

"You mean that shit with Deuce?"

"Yeah, that shit with Deuce. I'm good though. I came to grips with all that."

"Where you at?"

"I'll shoot you the address now."

Epilogue

Halo

December 2016 New Year's Eve

It was a little before midnight, and all of the family was together. After I hit True up and told him what the deal was, he came right away. I was a little nervous of what he might say or how he might act, but all that went away when my nigga walked in the door.

He was loaded down with all types of shit for Lil' Storm. I dapped my nigga up and cried at the same time. True was my brother for real. He didn't even hesitate to pack me and my kid up and take us back home. We stayed with him and Honesty in the house I had out in Romeoville.

True was doing good running Chicago. Shit was on the up and up. He got mad respect everywhere. When I finally decided to show my face, everybody was shocked because they thought something had happened to me. I just had to get right.

Sitting across from all my family as we sat in The Crystal Gardens Ballroom enjoying the last few minutes of 2016, this was it. This was the life, and life was good. I was missing Storm like crazy and knew if she was still here, we'd be living it up.

I know y'all probably thinking like how the fuck was we 'posed to have kids, right? Storm knew I was a lesbian the whole time. We had talked about kids before and knew that we'd do artificial insemination to have our family. That was the one thing we were adamant about. It was something that nobody knew but us.

Had she still been alive, we'd have at least one kid and one on the way by now. This whole time, that's all I could think about. I missed that woman with everything in me. Everything wasn't for everybody to know though, ya know?

Butta and Baby had twin boys that were born in March. They named them Brian Jr. and Brayden. They were now nine months old.

Bread's sons were growing so much. Both Brandon Jr. and Bryce were fully healed from their injuries and were now five-years-old. Bryce still cried for Brianna sometimes, but he was doing good. He was now three-years-old.

True and Honesty were still together even though True was on some fuck shit every now and then. I heard the arguments late at night between them, and that's when he'd actually come home. It got to be too much that I got my own spot and moved out. They would have to work that shit out.

As we got ready to countdown to the new year, I took one last look at my family. This right here was everything. I raised my glass while I held my baby girl in my arms. That shit shocked everybody too, but I still didn't get treated any different.

"10, 9, 8, 7, 6, 5, 4, 3, 2, 1. HAPPY NEW YEAR!!! I yelled. I toasted with everybody and hoped that 2017 brought all of us everything we needed.

The End

CPSIA information can be obtained
at www.ICGtesting.com
Printed in the USA
LVHW091759100219
607039LV00001B/13/P